MW00940935

Last Journey

A Gideon Johann Western
Book 6

By
Duane Boehm

Last Journey: A Gideon Johann Western Book 6

Copyright 2016 Duane Boehm

For more information or permission contact:
boehmduane@gmail.com

ISBN: 9781539711636

Other Books by Duane Boehm

In Just One Moment
Gideon Johann: A Gideon Johann Western Prequel
Last Stand: A Gideon Johann Western Book 1
Last Chance: A Gideon Johann Western Book 2
Last Hope: A Gideon Johann Western Book 3
Last Ride: A Gideon Johann Western Book 4
Last Breath: A Gideon Johann Western Book 5
Last Atonement: A Gideon Johann Western Book 7
Wayward Brother: A Gideon Johann Western Book 8
Where The Wild Horses Roam: Wild Horse Westerns Book 1
Spirit Of The Wild Horse: Wild Horse Westerns Book 2
Wild Horse On The Run: Wil Horse Westerns Book 3
What It All Comes Down To
Hand Of Fate: The Hand Of Westerns Book 1
Hand Of The Father: The Hand Of Westerns Book 2
Trail To Yesterday
Sun Over The Mountains
Wanted: A Collection of Western Stories (7 authors)
Wanted II: A Collection of Western Stories (7 authors)

Dedicated with love to Luna – the baby with the big brown eyes

Chapter 1

Sheriff Gideon Johann sat at his desk watching his son-in-law Zack Barlow as the young man took a seat across from him. Zack looked like hell. He was dark and puffy under the eyes, and his sunken in cheeks had changed his appearance. His mouth seemed to be in a permanent scowl and his brow always furrowed. After his weight loss, Zack's clothes hung on him like that of a homeless vagabond. He had been a strapping young man that now looked gaunt and poorly.

Zack had married Gideon's daughter Joann. She had been born out of wedlock and raised by her mother's aunt and uncle. Gideon had only learned of her existence after he returned to the town of Last Stand three years prior. In the interval, he had rekindled his relationship with Joann's mother Abby. The couple had married and now had a young son.

The last few months had been nothing but heartbreak for the Barlow and Johann families. Zack and Joann's daughter Tess had died in infancy, and then Joann had insisted on returning to the Wyoming Territory with her adoptive parents after they had come to Colorado for a visit. Everybody that Joann was close to, including both her real and adoptive parents, had tried to talk her out of leaving, but the headstrong, young woman would have none of it. Joann had insisted that she would never have another child. Before leaving, she told Zack that she loved him, but would not share a bed with him again, and the best way for her to avoid that temptation was to return to Wyoming.

Gideon felt as weary as Zack looked. He managed to keep his mind off the families' troubles during the day by staying busy, but at night when he went to bed, he found himself lying there for hours listening to his wife Abby snore while he worried about Joann and mourned the loss of his granddaughter. Tess's life had only lasted a couple of weeks, but Gideon had found himself drawn to the baby in a way that he couldn't even begin to describe. He missed her terribly. The absence of his free-spirit daughter left another void in his life. He and Joann had made up for a lot of lost time in the last three years. Life wasn't the same without her near him.

"What brings you to town?" Gideon asked.

"Gideon, I'm going to the Wyoming Territory. Joann's been gone a month and I've written her four times and not heard a word back. I can't take it any longer. I have to know something," Zack said as he leaned forward in his char.

"I planned to ride over tonight and tell you that Abby got a letter yesterday from her Aunt Rita," Gideon said.

"Really?" Zack interjected.

Abby had been forced by her parents to give Joann up at birth to her Aunt Rita and Uncle Jake. They had raised the child as their own in Wyoming.

"She wrote that Joann is doing all right and helping Uncle Jake with the ranch. The letter said that Joann won't mention anything to do with back here and that she's preoccupied with improving the ranch. Aunt Rita also said that Joann talks very little and is somber most of the time," Gideon said as he looked out the window towards the sound of the hammering.

A newcomer by the name of Cyrus Capello had arrived in Last Stand and had begun building a new saloon. Gideon had checked with other sheriffs in Colorado and learned that the saloon owner was a shady character that would leave a town to set up shop somewhere else when the law started breathing down his neck. Capello certainly looked the part of an Italian with his olive skin, Roman nose, bushy eyebrows, and dark greasy hair that he kept plastered down on his head. Cyrus liked to dress the role of a successful businessman with his frilly shirts and long coats. He stayed at the hotel as he supervised the building of his saloon. After the Last Stand Last Chance Saloon had gotten out of the whoring business, Gideon had feared that it was only a matter of time before supply and demand would lead to some entrepreneur filling the void. That day seemed to be close at hand.

"I guess she wants to forget about her life here," Zack said sadly.

"Zack, I imagine that not thinking about Last Stand is her way of coping. God knows we all talked until we were blue in the face to try to help her get past Tess's death. Nothing worked. I know it's hard to do, but you can't take her leaving personally. I know whence I speak. She's running from her pain just as I did. She's not really running from you."

Gideon had accidentally killed a young boy during the war and spent years running from his conscience. Only after returning to Last Stand had he been able to put the past behind him and move on with his life.

"I suppose so, but things feel kind of personal when my wife no longer wishes to live with me. Do you think I'm wrong to head up there?"

"No, I don't think you're wrong. I'm just not sure that you might not do more harm than good is all."

"Gideon, I just have to see Joann," Zack said, resignation in his voice.

"I understand. Are you going to take the train?"

"I think I'm going to ride up there. The hay is all in and sold, and I feel like being alone. Maybe by the time I get to Cheyenne, Joann will have a change of heart. I'm going to ride to Laramie and visit my aunt first."

"Don't you think it's a little late in the fall to be headed north?" Gideon questioned.

"I figured I'd ride east and go up the plains. I sure don't want to get snowed in going through a mountain pass."

"Well, I guess you can do what you want, but I think you should take the train," Gideon said, cringing a little as he heard his own words. Giving advice to Zack made him feel old. Somewhere along the way in the past couple of years, his life had taken on a fatherly role, and he couldn't stop himself from sharing his wisdom. The irony in his expecting someone to listen to his advice was not lost on Gideon and he begrudgingly smiled.

Deputy Finnegan Ford burst into the jail before the conversation could go any further. "We've got troubles. All the cowboys got paid today and have come to town. They've cornered one of those funny talking sheepherders that just moved here. He must have been buying supplies down at Hiram's store," Finnie said in his heavy Irish brogue.

"Calling somebody 'funny talking' is precious coming from you," Gideon said as he arose from his chair and headed to the gun rack.

"I'll have you know that people from Ireland were talking like this before there ever was a United States. My way of talking sounds a lot better than all that guttural growling like there's a chicken bone caught in your throat that your German ancestors did," Finnie said.

Gideon smiled as he handed Finnie a shotgun.

"Fatherhood is making you a touchy man," Gideon said.

Zack walked over to the gun rack and grabbed another shotgun. "I'm coming, too. You two might be so busy jawing at each other that you get yourselves shot," he said as he headed towards the door.

Four Basque sheepherders had moved into the area the previous month. The men were of an ancient race located in the Pyrenees Mountains between France and Spain, and recognized as some of the best sheepherders in the world. They were considered clannish and spoke their own language. Only one of the four men spoke any English whatsoever. They had brought about ten thousand sheep with them to graze the animals on open range. Their arrival had stirred up the local ranchers, but this was the first sign of trouble.

Gideon, Finnie, and Zack spread out as they neared the general store. There looked to be about ten ranch hands huddled around the sheepherder. They shoved and cursed the helpless man as they shouted and taunted him.

"Boys, unless you back away from that sheepherder, all your pay is going to go to Doc or the undertaker," Gideon called out.

The surprised ranch hands stopped and turned towards the sheriff. One of the men in the center of the crowd worked his way through the cowboys towards the sheriff. Gideon recognized him as the rancher, Lewis Wise.

"Sheriff, this isn't any of your concern. You were elected to serve by ranchers and the people of Last Stand. Not these squatters," Lewis said, contempt dripping from his voice.

"I was also sworn to uphold the law. You'd better leave that sheepherder alone. I don't care how big your ranch is," Gideon said testily.

"Sheriff, you know what they say about sheep – everything in front of them is eaten and everything behind is killed. I've heard tell that cattle will refuse to eat or drink on land soiled by sheep. We settled this land and have a right to protect it," Lewis argued.

"Lewis, you have no more right to the open range than those sheepherders do. I'm telling you that you'd better leave them alone. Now you and these cowboys can disperse or I'm arresting you for assault," Gideon said and cocked a barrel of the shotgun.

"Come on, boys. I'll buy you all a drink," Lewis said before marching off toward the Last Chance Saloon.

The sheepherder pulled a kerchief from his pocket and patted the blood off his busted lip. "Thank you, Sheriff," he said in halting English.

"Are you all right?" Gideon asked.

"I good. I no want trouble. We just try to raise our sheep."

"I'm Gideon Johann," Gideon said and offered his hand.

As the sheepherder shook hands with the sheriff, he said, "I'm Dominique Laxalt."

"Well, be careful, Dominique," Gideon said before turning to leave.

As the three men walked back to the jail, Finnie said, "Those sheepherders are going to put us in a pickle. I know we have to uphold the law, but if I were a rancher that settled this land against the Indians, I'd be a mite upset too if those smelly sheep started interfering with my way of life."

"I know. Believe me, I know," Gideon said as he carefully released the trigger on the shotgun.

Chapter 2

As Gideon rode home after the incident with the rancher and the sheepherder, he wondered what lay in store for the future. All of his work as a sheriff up to this point had been towards apprehending criminals. He had never butted up against what would be considered pillars of the community, and he tried to imagine how he would manage staying atop of the slippery slope of keeping the ranchers in line concerning the sheepherders.

Also troubling him was that come Monday, workers were to begin building a gallows for the hanging of Kurt Tanner the following Friday. The thought of carrying out the execution filled him with dread and made his stomach queasy. Killing someone that intended to do likewise was bad enough. He wanted no part in the proceedings. A professional hangman from Pueblo had been retained to carry out the sentence, but the sheriff would have to walk the prisoner up the gallows. Gideon wished that the event wouldn't become a public spectacle, but he knew otherwise. People loved a hanging. Kurt had been found guilty of killing two men. One while committing a robbery and another during his rustling spree. Two of his accomplices that worked for the Denver and Rio Grande Railroad had been sentenced to fifteen years in prison. A third man had received a five-year term for his part in the rustling in exchange for giving state's evidence.

Gideon arrived at his home and watched as his stepdaughter Winnie and his son Chance came running towards him. Seeing their smiling faces, he banished his worries from his mind and smiled at the two children. Chance had turned two-years-old earlier in the week, and he and his sister had begun to grabble for his attention and his ear.

"Me and Momma made you something today. Chance kind of helped. Guess what it is," Winnie said.

"Momma and I. You are not a simpleton. I bet you made me a new saddle," Gideon teased.

"No. I don't know how to make a saddle. Guess again," Winnie demanded.

"I bet you made me an apple pie."

"You guessed it," Winnie said with disappointment in her voice.

"Well, you asked me to guess," Gideon reminded the eleven-year-old as he climbed down from his horse.

Abby walked onto the porch of their cabin. "Quit your jawing and get in here. Supper is about ready," she announced.

Grinning, Gideon tipped his hat at his wife. "Yes, ma'am."

Abby had her arm hooked around one of the porch pillars with her body leaning away as if she were going to swing on the pole. The pose made her look like a carefree teenager. Sometimes Gideon still needed to pinch himself to believe that he was married to his first love after all the years they had spent apart. He thought Abby got prettier every year. She had come through the death of Tess and the departure of Joann better than anyone else had, but at times, he could see the losses weighing on his wife. Most of the evenings spent in their home were not as lively as they had been in the past.

At the dinner table, Gideon told Abby about Zack's plans for traveling to Wyoming.

"Did you try to talk him out of it?" Abby asked.

"No, not really. Do you think I should have?" Gideon asked.

"I don't know. I don't think he will be well received. You know how headstrong that girl is, and she did leave to get away from Zack. But then again, she is your daughter and I doubt that she puts this behind her without some prodding from somebody."

Gideon managed to smile at his wife. His wife's words couldn't have been truer. If he hadn't ended up back in Last Stand too near death to run, he would still be out there somewhere running from his past. Only through the love and caring of his friends and Abby had he been able to move on with his life.

Red, their dog, started barking and growling. Gideon jumped up from the table and peeked out the window. He could see five riders approaching. At first, he grabbed his Winchester rifle, and then thought better of it. He reached for the shotgun above the door and checked its loads.

"Everybody stay at the table while I see what these visitors want. It's probably nothing," Gideon instructed as he headed out the door.

Standing on the porch, he cradled the shotgun in his arm. As the riders neared the cabin, Gideon recognized Lewis Wise, the rancher he'd had the encounter with earlier in the day, and four other area ranchers. Sighing, he allowed himself to relax a little. He didn't expect violence from the men, but knew the visit was no social call either. The ranchers rode into the yard and stopped in front of the cabin.

"Evening, Sheriff," Lewis called out.

"What's this all about, Lewis?" Gideon asked, forsaking the pleasantries.

"I got together with some of the other ranchers this afternoon and we felt it necessary to impress upon you our concerns regarding the sheepherders. You bought heifers from some of us this fall and will be needing more of the open range yourself. We don't wish to do anybody harm, but all of our livelihoods are at stake here."

"I didn't get the impression that you were too concerned with whether you harmed that sheepherder in town."

"One of the boys got a little rambunctious. I don't condone his actions, but I still find it troubling that you take up for those foreigners over us citizens that helped make this country what it is."

"I see," Gideon said and shifted his weight from one leg to the other. "I'm not sure what you think this meeting is supposed to accomplish. Like I already told you, I'm sworn to uphold the law, and that's what I aim to do. Citizenship has nothing to do with anything. I may not be thrilled with sheep running all over the place either, but those sheepherders have the same rights that you and I have. You best listen up when I tell you that I'm going to enforce the law and I don't care where that leads. Frank DeVille used to be the biggest rancher around. He thought he was above the law and he's dead now. Secondly, why didn't you come see me at my office?"

"By the time that we got organized, you'd left for the day. We thought it necessary to convey our sense of urgency immediately," Lewis said.

"This is my home and I have small children here. You may remember that crazy preacher and his men already tried to harm them. Riders showing up tend to make us nervous. If any of you ever show up out here again for any reason other than a social visit, I'm going to take it real personal. Real personal. I hope I make myself clear," Gideon said.

"I hope we've all made ourselves real clear," Lewis said before turning his horse and riding away with the others in tow.

After walking back into the cabin, Gideon returned to his meal. "Just some ranchers out scouting grazing spots and stopped in to say hello."

Abby eyed her husband and knew that he had lied in order not to scare Winnie. Gideon made eye contact with her and winked with his devilish grin.

∞

The ranchers left the Johann homestead in an agitated state and decided to head to town to have a drink at the Last Chance. Packed with the usual Friday night crowd of ranch hands, the men could find no empty seats in the saloon. Some cowboys that worked for the ranchers offered their table and the five men sat down at it.

Mary, the owner of the saloon, stood behind the bar helping fill mugs of beer while trying to carry on a conversation with her husband Deputy Ford. The couple had lived above the saloon until recently when the birth of their son had necessitated buying a house close to the saloon. Mary had hired a widow lady and moved her into their spare bedroom to tend to the baby when neither she nor Finnie could be home.

"What do you think that is all about?" Mary asked as she nodded her head toward the table of ranchers.

Finnie turned his head to look. "Gideon had a run-in with Lewis today over one of those sheepherders. I would imagine it would have something to do with that."

"You better get home. I imagine Mrs. Penny has about had her fill of babysitting Sam for one day. I've only been able to get home long enough to feed him. It's been a busy day."

Finnie took his leave and Mary walked over to the table of ranchers.

"What brings some of Last Stand's finest out tonight?" Mary asked.

"We'll have a round of beers," Lewis said.

Mary motioned for Delta to bring the drinks.

Carter Mason began twisting the end of his handlebar mustache before he spoke. "Mary, I know that Gideon is a friend of yours, and that Finnie is his deputy, but that sheriff is about the most hardheaded man I've ever come across in my life. We paid him a visit to talk about the sheepherders and he didn't appreciate our calling on him. We're all just trying to look out for our livelihoods."

"That's Gideon for you. Being honorable doesn't always go hand in hand with pragmatic," Mary said, trying to sound cheery.

Delta brought the tray of drinks and Mary passed them around to the men.

Lewis took a sip of beer before he said, "I sure hope that sheriff understands the weight we carry in the community. As well as he's served this town, it'd be a shame to lose him."

Mary placed her palms on the table and leaned over closer to the men. "Gentlemen, I appreciate your business and all, but if any of you think you're man enough to take on Gideon, you're sadly mistaken. He'd chew you up and spit you out like a piece of gristle," she said before whisking away towards the bar.

The men eyed one another, but said nothing before resuming their drinking.

After a couple more rounds of beer, Lewis said, "I know where those sheepherders make camp. What do you say to kicking in two hundred dollars apiece and offering them the thousand dollars just to move along out of here? I have the money on me and you can pay me later. It could be money well spent."

The other four men nodded their heads in agreement before walking out of the saloon and saddling up. They rode northeast out of town towards where the sheepherders made camp. The sound of sheep bleating drifted across the still night and reached the men before they could actually see the flock. By the time they spotted the sheep, the herding dogs were raising a ruckus to alert their masters of the ranchers' arrival.

As the ranchers rode into camp, they found the four Basque sheepherders standing by their wagon with only two shotguns to go around. Their dogs stood by their sides, growling and barking at the riders. The sheepherders looked nervous in the firelight as they exchanged glances amongst themselves and then towards the ranchers.

"We mean you no harm. We only came to talk," Lewis called out before dismounting.

Dominique, the man accosted in town that day, stepped forward. "What you want?" he asked in broken English.

"This is cattle country and we want to keep it that way. We came to offer you one thousand dollars to move on out of here. Go another sixty miles to the northeast. There's good land in that direction. You can make some quick money and still have good land to graze your flock."

Turning to the three other sheepherders, Dominique began speaking to them in Euskera. The conversation soon became heated with Dominique and two of the others arguing vehemently with the fourth man. Lewis looked over his shoulder at the other ranchers, not sure what to make of the situation.

Finally, Dominique turned towards the ranchers. He still brandished the shotgun in a casual manner, but had moved his thumb to the hammer. "My brothers and I have decided. We will not leave. We like here. Moved too many times. No more running."

Lewis adjusted his hat and stared at Dominique. "I see," he said. "We've made you a good offer and you should've taken it. I fear you'll come to regret this day. Some ranchers are a lot meaner than me."

Andrew Stallings climbed down from his horse. The rancher seldom drank and the few beers had washed away his usual reserved nature. He staggered a little as he marched towards the sheepherder and shoved him.

"You smell like sheep dung and if you think we're going to sit here while you ruin our land and livelihood you have another thing coming," Andrew yelled into Dominique's face.

Lewis grabbed Andrew and pulled him away from the sheepherder.

"There's no call for that tonight. Give these men time to sleep on our offer and they may see things differently in the light of day," Lewis said.

"They damn well better. I know a cottonwood with a limb that would support four nooses just fine," Andrew yelled.

"You leave. We no fear you. Go," Dominique ordered.

Shoving Andrew back to his horse, Lewis climbed onto his mount. He turned toward the other ranchers. "Let's go home. This will be solved one way or the other. No need to lose any sleep over things," he said before riding away.

Chapter 3

As Zack looked around the cabin that he had finished building for Joann the previous spring, he thought about all that had already transpired in the home. His and Joann's only child had been born and died within the confines of the still new walls. A lot of good times had also taken place in the short time that they had lived there, and he allowed himself to smile at the memories of some of the more risqué moments. He glanced at the photograph sitting on the mantel that he and Joann had made at the time of their wedding. In the photo, Joann's mischievous grin had captured the very essence of his wife. He wondered if she would ever smile like that again or if he would ever share another picture with her. Zack reached down and ran his fingers along the arm of the rocking chair that he had surprised his wife with after Tess's birth. After the baby's death, Joann had rocked for hours at a time in a near catatonic state until the floorboards were polished slick from the friction of wood on wood. He made a final glance around the room, having reminisced all that he could stand. After snatching up his stuffed saddlebags, he marched out the door and mounted his horse. He planned to visit Tess's grave before he began his journey to the Wyoming Territory.

Tess lay buried beside Gideon's mother on the Johann homestead. Zack arrived at Gideon's place and scanned the yard, surprised not to see any of the family outdoors on a Saturday morning. He tied his horse and walked through the gate into the little cemetery. Grass had begun to get a foothold on covering the bare dirt of the grave and the sight gave him pause. The world had kept right on spinning as if his daughter had never existed and the notion made him feel more melancholy than he already did. He leaned down and traced Tess's name on the tombstone with his finger.

"Tess, I'm going to be gone for a while and I'll think of you every day. I'm going to go try to get your momma back. She missed you so much that she couldn't stand to be here anymore, but I need her," he said before having to stop. Tears welled up in his eyes and he took a big gulp of air before continuing. "Daddy misses his little girl."

Abby walked out onto the porch to pitch a bucket of dirty water she'd used to mop the floors. She spied Zack and waited patiently until he walked out of the graveyard before she headed towards her son-in-law. Zack made a quick swipe of his sleeve across his eyes when he saw Abby coming.

"I hear that you're going to be leaving us for a while," Abby said.

"Abby, I have to try to get her back," Zack said.

"I know you do."

"Back when Joann and I were courting and she was giving me fits, I should've known that she was nothing but trouble and run for the hills. Everybody should have just come out and told me that I was no match for her."

Abby gave Zack a maternal smile. "I don't believe that for a minute and I don't think you do either. You two were great for each other and then life handed you a tragedy that Joann couldn't cope with. She has a lot of her daddy in her. They try to run from their pain. She'll eventually figure out that there's no running from it, but I don't know how long that may take."

"I feel so empty. We should have been there for each other. Isn't that what marriage is all about?" Zack said and tried to smile.

"Yes, you're right, but there wasn't any reasoning with that girl. Just remember that her imprudent ways were part of the reason you fell in love with her in the first place," Abby said.

"I guess I better get started. I've got a long ride."

"Zack, you know that I love you every bit as much as I do Joann. You be careful on your journey. I'll be worrying until you get back."

Zack leaned over and hugged his mother-in-law. "Thank you. I love you, too."

"Gideon is checking on the herd and the kids are inside the cabin. Do you want to tell them goodbye?" Abby asked.

"I don't think I can handle seeing Winnie and Chance today. I just want to ride."

"I understand," she said as she watched Zack mount his horse. "Send us a telegram when you get there."

"Will do. Bye, Abby."

Zack headed east. He planned to ride in that direction until he passed the last of the mountain ranges and reached the plains before heading north. Many a mile stood between him and his destination. Apprehension over the likely reception he'd receive when we he saw Joann made him nearly nauseous and sent a chill up his spine. He pulled his coat shut against the cool fall air. Back before he met Joann, he considered his life a lonely existence, but those days didn't hold a candle to the keen sense of solitude he felt now with Tess and his wife no longer in his life.

∞

Joann, covered in a fine coat of dust, walked into the ranch home where she had been born and raised. Only her height and slim build hinted at her hidden femininity. She wore men's trousers with suspenders, a work shirt, and had her hair tucked up under her hat.

Her adoptive mother, standing over the cooking stove fixing supper, looked over at her daughter. "Joann, what am I going to do with you? You need to come in the back door and shed those clothes before you go traipsing through my clean house. I raised you better than that," she said.

Ignoring her mother's request, Joann said, "We need a rain. I probably gained a pound from swallowing dust today, but we got the herd sorted."

"Where's your poppa?"

"He's tending to the horses. He said I'd done enough for one day and sent me to the house."

Taking a seat at the table, her mother said, "Come sit down with me."

"What is it, Momma?" Joann asked as she walked towards the table.

"We need to talk," her momma said and cringed as she watched the dust sift off her daughter with each step.

Plopping into a chair, Joann said, "Momma, I'm a grown woman now. I can fend for myself just fine."

"You're the daughter and I'm the momma, and it will be that way until they plant me in the ground. I don't care how old you are so you best listen. We've avoided this conversation long enough. Joann, you have a husband and a home back in Colorado. You can't go on acting as if you don't. Pretending doesn't make it so. You made a vow before the eyes of God to Zack, and you need to honor it. Zack needs you and you need him. You're fooling yourself if you think that by coming here you've put all your hurt behind you. Hurt doesn't go away until it's made you bear its full weight," her momma said.

Joann sat up straight in her chair and her eyes narrowed. She didn't appreciate being talked to as if she were a little girl and a foolish one to boot. "I did plenty of hurting from the time Tess died until I came here. I hurt so much that I thought I'd lost my mind. Coming here wasn't running. It was deciding to start a new life. You always said that I was so independent that you pitied the man I would marry. I've come to realize that you were right. I'm too independent to be married. I should have never left home and gone to Colorado. I belong here with you and Poppa. Momma, I'm not a child anymore. I know what I want," she said defiantly.

Her mother picked up an apple from a bowl on the table and began rolling the fruit in her fingers. "So you don't miss Zack then?"

Looking towards the window, Joann's eyes began to moisten. The tears welled up before leaking over the rims and making trails through the dust on her cheeks. She took her hands and swiped the moisture away, smearing her face with mud in the process. "Zack was a mistake. Poor Tess was even a bigger mistake. I swear I'll never make either of them again."

"You sound like a silly schoolgirl. I had more than my fair share of disappointments in trying to have a baby. If I let it do to me what it has to you, I never would have been willing to raise you. And where would either of us be then? God had a plan for us to be a family. You know how much I love you, but I'm telling you that this denial will catch up with you before it's over. And that's a promise."

Joann popped the table with her fist. Her voice sounded shrill with rage as she spoke. "I know you had disappointments, but you never gave birth to a child and you never had that child die in your arms. I died inside that day, too. And don't talk to me about God. What kind of God takes a little helpless baby's life? I just want to live here with you and Poppa in peace and help run the ranch. Please do me that favor," she yelled.

Looking towards the door, Joann noticed her poppa had entered the house.

"Rita, what's going on?" he asked his wife.

"We're just having a girl talk. Go on and get cleaned up, Jake. Everything is fine here," Rita answered.

Jake looked curiously at his wife before heading to the back of the house, causing his wife to grimace as more dust floated to the floor.

Rita studied her daughter and waited until her husband had walked out of hearing range. "You can paint things anyway that you want, but from where I sit, it looks as though you're running from your problems just like your natural father did. Now calm yourself down. There's no call for such outbursts."

Joann looked her mother in the eyes. She had forgotten how bullheaded her momma could be when she was sure that she was in the right. "I'm not running like Daddy . . ." she said before pausing. Addressing Gideon as Daddy still made her uncomfortable in front of her parents. "Like he did. I'm not going anywhere. I've decided to make a life here."

"I need to get back to cooking, but I make no promises to keep quiet. I'm still your momma," Rita reminded her daughter again as she arose from her chair. She paused and started to laugh. "You should see your face. You look as if you've put on war paint."

"Good. Somebody could get scalped before the night is through," Joann said and allowed herself the faintest of smiles.

Chapter 4

Between the hammering on the new saloon and the construction of the gallows, Gideon had about all the noise he could stand. For three days, he'd listened to the relentless racket coming from both sides of the jail. The thought of overseeing the hanging already had him on edge and the banging added to his anxiety.

Gideon strolled into the cell room to check on Kurt Tanner. The prisoner was asleep as usual. Kurt had begun taking respite from his impending death with naps. About the only time he wasn't lying down was to eat his meals on the rare occasion that he had an appetite. Since the sentencing, he barely spoke when awake.

As Gideon walked back into his office, he noticed that the hammering on the gallows side had stopped. Before he could walk to the window, one of the carpenters entered the jail.

"Sheriff, we have your gallows finished," the carpenter said.

"Believe me, I lay no claim to it. Would you be so kind as to go to the hotel and inform Mr. Wells that he can test that thing whenever he wants? Please make yourself available to him in case he needs adjustments. And bring me an invoice when you're finished," Gideon said.

"Sure, Sheriff," the carpenter said before leaving.

A short time later, Cyrus Capello, the owner of the saloon under construction, walked into the jail. Gideon had only met the man one other time when he made his usual introduction to new inhabitants of Last Stand.

"Sheriff, may I have a moment of your time?" Cyrus asked.

"Sure, have a seat," Gideon answered.

"I wanted to let you know that the saloon will be finished momentarily. You won't have to listen to all of that racket much longer. The timing of the completion has worked out exquisitely. I received a telegram early this morning that my supplies and employees are in Alamosa and should reach Last Stand later today. That will give us tomorrow to get our house in order and then have our grand opening after the hanging. I would think we should have a good crowd on hand."

"I fear you're right about that. I'd prefer this not to turn into a spectacle."

"We have to agree to disagree on that. Folks enjoy a good hanging and I intend to provide them recreation afterwards," Cyrus said.

"I don't suppose there are any laws against it," Gideon remarked.

"Officers of the law are always welcome at the Pearl West Saloon for drinks or whatever pleasures they desire – all on the house. We like to stay on favorable terms with the sheriff and his men."

"I'll remember that, Mr. Capello. I might stop in for a drink, but I don't think my wife would appreciate me partaking of any other pleasures," Gideon said and smiled.

"Call me Cyrus. We have a back door for those seeking indiscretion, Sheriff."

"I'll pass. And Cyrus, I hope you realize that we have a nice little peaceful town here and I won't hesitate to keep it that way," Gideon warned.

"Don't you worry about a thing," Cyrus said before turning his head at the sound of the door closing.

Finnie walked into the jail and froze at the sight of the new saloon owner. He'd kept his distance from Cyrus upon learning of the new man's intentions to open a saloon. Even the idea of speaking to Cyrus felt like disloyalty towards his wife and her establishment.

"Finnie, come on in and meet Cyrus Capello. You two are bound to cross paths at some point and it might as well be now," Gideon said to end Finnie's awkwardness concerning the situation.

Cyrus stood and held out his hand. "Good to meet you, sir. I understand your wife owns the Last Stand Last Chance Saloon. I admire a woman with a keen business sense. I wish you and yours no harm and hope you do the same for me. I think you'll see that both saloons can survive each other's existence. In fact, I think you'll find us good for your business. From past experience, I've found that two saloons tend to draw more people to town. These cowboys convince themselves that there's double the pleasure waiting for them."

Finnie shook the man's hand and looked at him warily. Seldom did he cross paths with a man that could outtalk him, but he realized he'd met his match. "Good to meet you. May our profits flow as free as your tongue."

Cyrus grinned and Gideon attempted to stymie a snort. The hammering had stopped and the jail had gone quiet for the first time in weeks.

"From the sound of things, or I should say the lack thereof, I believe my saloon is completed. Gentlemen, I have business to tend. Good day," Cyrus said before exiting.

Dropping into a chair, Finnie said, "I don't believe a word that dago said. You can smell trouble on that man like a fart after a bean supper. We should drag him down to the livery and let Blackie use the grease from Cyrus's hair to lubricate a wagon axle."

Gideon chuckled. "We'll have to keep an eye on him for sure, but I expect you're right."

"Of course, I'm right. As sure as you can find girls working in a whorehouse."

"I think we'll be having those girls arriving this afternoon."

"I don't blame Mary for getting out of the whoring trade, but I always knew that someday somebody would take our place. I sure hope they don't run us out of business," Finnie said.

"I'm sure they'll take some of your business, but I don't think you'll have to worry about being ruined."

"Let's go over to the Last Chance and have lunch. All this conjecturing has stirred my hunger," Finnie said as he stood.

After lunch, Gideon walked out of the saloon just as the hangman tested the gallows with a sack of rocks substituting for the intended victim. The sound of the trapdoor dropping open sent a shiver through the sheriff and he rubbed the scar on his cheek out of habit as he always did when agitated. From atop the platform, the hangman spotted the sheriff and smiled before giving a thumb up sign.

Gideon spent the rest of the day in his office reviewing wanted posters and doing paperwork. Late in the afternoon, Doc Abram walked into the jail. The old doctor was as much a fixture in Last Stand as the mountains standing in the background. Shuffling to a chair across from Gideon, Doc plopped down and pulled off his spectacles.

Gideon leaned back in his chair and said, "You've made yourself scarce."

"I've had a stream of patients since I opened the door this morning. I don't just get to sit at my desk all day pretending I'm busy," Doc said.

Grinning, Gideon said, "Save your rancor for Finnie. This hanging already has me riled."

"I've yet to receive a response from the advertising I did back east for a new doctor. You would think there would be at least a couple of freshly graduated physicians that would want to come experience life out west. Maybe they're all getting soft and citified."

"So you're really going to bring in a new doctor and start cutting back on your hours?"

"I am if I can find someone I can tolerate and I think will fit in well here. Ever since Sheriff Fuller retired, he's been hounding me to take up fishing with him and I'm ready. I also want to take that trip to Boston to see those grandkids," Doc said.

"I've never seen a curmudgeon go so soft over meeting his grandchildren one time," Gideon teased.

Doc rubbed his chin and turned reflective. "You know what I'm talking about. I still think about whether I could have done something different to save Tess. Your granddaughter's death still grieves me."

Finnie burst through the door causing both men to jump. "You should see the procession heading into town," he said.

"Damn, Finnie, you could scare an old man to death," Doc said irritably.

"You'll still be here aggrieving us all long after the mountains have worn away," Finnie retorted.

The three men walked outside and sat down on the bench outside of the jail to watch as the wagon train arrived. Wagons passed by with kegs of beer, crates of liquor, tables, game boards, chairs, and lastly a covered wagon with the side flaps pulled up. Inside the covered wagon were four girls dressed more scantily than Gideon had ever seen in any saloon he had ever frequented. The girls flashed their titties at the three men as the wagon passed by while giggling and blowing kisses.

"Oh, my. The Last Chance may never have another customer after that place opens," Finnie said, taking off his hat and running his hand through his hair.

"I have a suspicion that I'll be treating a lot more gunshot wounds and French pox," Doc remarked.

Gideon didn't say anything, but watched the wagons pass all the way down Last Stand's main street, go around the final block, and return through town until they reached the front of the new establishment. Cyrus Capello stood in the entrance of the Pearl West greeting the new arrivals.

"Finnie, I fear we're about to really start earning our pay," Gideon said before standing and walking back into the jail.

Chapter 5

On the Thursday night before the hanging, Gideon slept fitfully. The tossing and turning had almost gotten him evicted from his own bed after waking Abby for the third time. Joann and Zack had been on his mind when he laid down, and then he started thinking about Tess before finally fretting over the hanging scheduled for the following day. The thought of marching Kurt Tanner up the steps of the gallows to the murderers own death nearly nauseated him. He wondered if he had it to do over if he would've just killed Kurt during the outlaw's capture. A quick death with a bullet seemed preferable to all the waiting to be hanged. Kurt had lost so much weight that the sheriff worried that the young man's neck might not snap. Gideon had never witnessed a hanging, but had heard tales of outlaws flopping at the end of a rope for fifteen minutes as they strangled to death.

After rising earlier than usual, Gideon had breakfast cooked by the time Abby and the children arose. The meal turned out to be a quiet affair as everybody seemed to mimic Gideon's unusual silence and somberness.

Abby handed her husband his hat. "Gideon, you're just doing your job," she said.

"Oh, I know. Doesn't make it any less daunting of a task though," he said as he ran his hand through his hair before putting on his hat.

"I suppose not."

"I'll probably sleep at the jail tonight. I expect a big crowd in town and the new saloon is opening afterward. Should make for a lively day," he said before kissing Abby and heading out the door.

The hanging had been scheduled for noon and people were already arriving in town by the time that Gideon rode down the street. The café that Finnie and Mary had opened didn't look to have an empty seat and the town merchants had opened early for the occasion. Gideon walked into the jail to find Finnie pouring coffee.

"Top of the morning to you," the Irishman greeted him.

"Morning. Looks like a hanging is good business for everybody but Kurt. You couldn't get served at your own restaurant right now," Gideon said.

"People certainly have a morbid curiosity. We've seen enough death to last us a lifetime. Changes one's point of view," Finnie said as he handed Gideon a cup.

"That it does. How's Kurt?"

Finnie shook his head. "Not good. He won't eat. He's afraid of messing himself."

Gideon dropped into his chair and tossed down his hat. "Let's make some extra trips through town. There'll be a lot of people and more chance for something to happen."

"I'll make a round as soon as I finish this coffee," Finnie said before taking a sip.

Ethan Oakes arrived at the jail just before ten in the morning. He and Gideon had been best friends since childhood. Even an eighteen-year lapse with no communications whatsoever had failed to weaken their bond. Ethan ranched through the week and preached on Sunday. Kurt Tanner had been his ranch hand before being arrested.

"I thought I'd stop by to administer to Kurt's spiritual needs and see if I could be of some small comfort," Ethan said to Gideon.

"Have at it, but I'm not sure what kind of reception you'll receive. If he doesn't want comforting, I sure could use some. I wish I had no part in these proceedings," Gideon said as he looked up from his desk at his towering friend.

Ethan removed his gun belt and walked towards the cell room as Gideon followed with the key. Kurt sat on the edge of his bed staring down at the floor. He never bothered looking up at the sound of the men entering the room.

"Kurt, I've come to see if I could sit and talk with you. Maybe we could pray together," Ethan said.

Kurt jumped up from the bed and threw his hands in the air. "You want to talk? It's a little late for that now, don't you think? I never knew you to take much interest in me when I worked by your side. Why now?" he yelled.

In a measured tone, Ethan said, "I believed you were a young man trying to find his way and I didn't want to come off as heavy-handed in my dealings with you. You never struck me as being too interested in what I had to say anyway. When appropriate, I tried to offer advice, and I certainly made a point to always be friendly toward you. You made your choices on your own accord and will have to pay for them. I'm here to tend to your spiritual needs."

"You came from a fine family and have no idea what my life was like as a kid. You learn to take to survive. I make no apologies for my actions. Now get out of here," Kurt shouted.

Ethan looked down at the floor and then up at Kurt. "Please allow me to help you," he pleaded.

"Get the hell out of here. It's all a lie anyways," Kurt screamed before turning towards the window and staring out at the gallows.

Walking out of the room, Ethan took a seat across from the desk. Gideon shut the cell room door and sat down in his chair.

"You all right?" Gideon asked.

"Oh, yeah. Maybe I could've offered Kurt more guidance along the way, but I feared pushing him away. I've developed a sense for when people are ready to find faith and Kurt never struck me as being close. And you and I always had our misgivings about his character in the first place. Maybe I never believed in him enough to make an effort and that's a failing on my part, but I won't accept any responsibility for his actions. He certainly knew right from wrong," Ethan said with resignation.

"I'll just be glad when this is over," Gideon said and rubbed his scar.

"Sometimes I wonder about the legitimacy of hanging someone. Does any man, even an officer of the court, have the right to condemn another of God's children to death? Is that really any different than what the criminal did to receive such a sentence?"

"Ethan, I don't want to think about such things at this moment. I'm having a hard enough time with my part in all this without bringing religion into things," Gideon said with exasperation.

"You're right. I was only thinking out loud. Time for me to head home. I won't be an audience to this like it is some minstrel show in town."

"I'll see you Sunday. We need to get our wives to plan a get together with our families along with Finnie and Mary for a meal after church. It's time to get back to living and have some fun. We've mourned enough that we could use some laughter."

"See you then. And be strong. You're only doing your sworn job," Ethan said before leaving.

Finnie entered the jail at eleven-thirty. "You should see the crowd out there. They're as thick as a whorehouse with a two-for-one sale. Even women and children. Not my idea of entertainment."

Gideon glanced over at the clock. "Did you talk to that hangman, Mr. Wells?"

"Yeah. He told me he'd take his station at five 'til noon. You are to walk Tanner up to the noose and he will take it from there," Finnie answered as he took a seat.

The two men sat fidgeting with papers, watches, and anything else they could find to occupy their minds. Neither spoke. Gideon had never seen Finnie go so long without talking in the jail. He thought about teasing the Irishman just to get him riled and talking to relieve the tension, but decided against the notion.

At eleven-fifty, Gideon pulled his handcuffs out of the drawer. "Grab your rifle. Let's get our prisoner ready," he said as he arose to his feet.

Kurt Tanner looked up as the lawmen walked into the room. The sight of the two men caused him to send projectile vomit across the cell. He dropped to his knees and puked until he had the dry heaves.

Gideon waited until Tanner had stopped before opening the cell door. "Kurt, the last image everyone will have of you is how you chose to die. Try to be strong and let them remember you as someone that was brave and took your sentence like a man. Your death will be talked about for a long time. You control how the story will go," he said. His voice lacked conviction, but he didn't know what else to say.

Tanner stood and meekly held out his arms. He didn't speak as Gideon cuffed him. Finnie led the way as the prisoner followed and Gideon brought up the rear. The Irishman had to clear a path through the swarm of bystanders to reach the gallows. He ascended the stairs and Kurt Tanner followed without hesitation. Once they reached the scaffold, Finnie stood to the side as the sheriff led Tanner to the noose.

Gideon looked out over the crowd – a virtual sea of humanity or maybe inhumanity. Last Stand had never had this many people in the town and he wondered how far some of them had traveled. He could feel sweat run from his armpits down his side even though he felt chilled. After pulling a piece of paper from his pocket, Gideon read the sentence proclamation. He asked Tanner if he had any last words and the prisoner shook his head without speaking.

The hangman walked over and placed a black hood over Tanner's head. He then placed the noose around Kurt's neck and adjusted it to his satisfaction before retreating back to the trapdoor lever. Without hesitating, he pulled the wooden arm. The door clanked open and Kurt Tanner disappeared from sight as the crowd let out a collective gasp.

Gideon peeked through the trap opening and could see that the drop had broken Kurt's neck and that the prisoner hung lifeless. He glanced over at Finnie. His deputy looked as pale as a ghost, and Gideon guessed that he probably looked the same.

As the body of Kurt Tanner still twitched and twisted on the rope, somebody shouted out in a booming voice, "The Pearl West is officially open for business. Everything, and I mean everything, is half-price for our grand opening. Come in and experience one of the finest saloons west of the Mississippi."

The crowd began dispersing in every direction. Looking down from the scaffold, Gideon thought all the people looked like a stampeding herd on a cattle drive. Finnie walked up beside him and watched.

"What now?" Finnie asked.

"The cabinetmaker, or I guess I should say the undertaker, is supposed to take care of the body. He'll probably start charging the county more now that he's had some training. I fear we'll be busy tonight," Gideon answered.

"I need to take a walk to gather myself and then I'll clean up that puke in the cell. I don't have an appetite anyway," Finnie said before turning and walking down the steps.

By five o'clock, the population of Last Stand had thinned out considerably, but the streets were still crowded with more people than usual even for a Friday evening. A nervous energy ran through the town as if the hanging had put people on edge rather than give them pause to reflect on their actions in life. Gideon stuck his head in the Pearl West before walking to the Last Chance. Both places were packed shoulder to shoulder with men drinking and having a good time. Mary spotted him from behind the bar and gave a little wave. Not wishing to fight the crowd, Gideon walked to Mary's Place, the café that Mary and Finnie had opened. He found an unoccupied table and sat down at it.

Charlotte, the waitress, came to the table. She liked to play an adversarial role with Gideon and Finnie even though she owed her current state of affairs to their assistance.

"The town is busting at the seams with people and you're eating alone. That could make a man take stock of his popularity within the community," Charlotte said.

"Why would I want company when I have you to regale me with insults?" Gideon asked.

"Don't start using big words with me. I could make your food taste less than pleasing."

"And I might haul you back to Cecil Hobbs and tell him that you two are legally married after all."

Grinning at the sheriff, Charlotte said, "You are a haughty man, Gideon Johann. Are you going to order or would you rather spend your time threatening a poor defenseless maiden?"

"I'll have a beefsteak cooked medium with some greens and a cup of tea, if it so pleases the lady."

"I'll take your order out of respect for Mary's good name and not out of a threat from the likes of you," Charlotte said before heading to the kitchen.

When Charlotte returned with Gideon's meal, she sat down across from the sheriff.

"Are you all right? I would imagine the hanging has to be heavy on your mind," she said.

Gideon forced himself to suppress smiling at the young woman. Charlotte normally hid her true nature in a barrage of insults, and he didn't want her to think he was making light of her concerns.

"I appreciate your concerns and I do hope I never have to take part in a hanging again," Gideon answered before falling silent. He wasn't quite sure how to carry on a conversation with Charlotte without insults flying.

"I'll let you eat in peace. I just wanted to check on you since I know your wife is at home and Mary is too busy to talk," she said before standing.

"Thank you, Charlotte. I would be a mess without women looking out for me," he said with a wink as a customer beckoned the waitress away.

The meal proved tasty and Gideon ate slowly to appreciate the food and to kill time. Too many hours of the day were still left to occupy his time before the saloons shut down for the night. He contemplated going home and leaving Finnie to look after the town, but his instincts told him that both of them would be needed before the night ended. With the swallow of his last bite of food, Gideon walked to the counter and paid for his meal before heading towards the jail.

Finnie and Doc sat in front of the building. Gideon could see that they were having some kind of lively debate before he could hear them.

Turning towards the sheriff, Doc said, "Not only is your deputy good at upholding the law, but he is an expert on the medical profession as well. He's trying to tell me what kind of doctor I need to hire."

"I just said that it'd be good if a new doctor came from out west so he wouldn't be shocked about how life is out here like somebody from the east would be. Doc puffed up like a toad and started telling me his life story about moving out west and how he adjusted just fine," Finnie said in defense.

Gideon looked at the two men and realized that he was expected to choose a side. He couldn't care less about their argument. His only decision was to pick which one of his two friends that he wanted to gang up on. "Finnie is right. Somebody from west of the Mississippi wouldn't have to adjust to our ways. Doc, you might have been able to develop a better bedside manner if you hadn't spent all that time getting used to the west."

Finnie let out a chortle.

Doc slapped his leg and pulled off his spectacles. "You two are hilarious. If either one of you is ever injured again, I'm going to castrate you while I got you on the table. The world doesn't need any more children from the loins of the likes of you two jugheads. I haven't even had a response from out east. How do either of you think I could find somebody in the west? Doctors don't exactly grow on trees out here, you know."

"And I won't name any more of my children after you if you're going to talk like that," Finnie said.

"Keep talking and I'll make a steer out of you before this night is through," Doc said.

"Scoot over you two and I'll sit in the middle to keep the peace. I'm sure Doc will find us a suitable doctor. Let's talk about women. I'm sure we can all agree on what a mystery they all are," Gideon said.

The three men remained sitting outside the jail for the next couple of hours shooting the breeze until Doc left to go home. Both saloons were still going strong and the doctor decided to forgo his usual beer drinking at the Last Chance after hearing all of the hooting and hollering drifting down the street.

Gideon and Finnie took turns strolling down Main Street and back again. The patrons at both saloons had managed to behave themselves and the two men grew bored with nothing to do but sit.

As ten o'clock neared, Gideon said, "Maybe I wasted our time tonight. I had a feeling there'd be trouble. Could be I'm getting paranoid in my old age."

"The evening's not over. The cowboys should just be getting liquored up good about now. I just hope if there's trouble that it's at the new place and not the Last Chance," Finnie remarked.

Twenty minutes later, a woman screamed from inside the Pearl West. Men started yelling and jeering, and some could be seen by the light of the streetlamps making a hasty exit out the front door.

The two lawmen ran for the saloon, pushing people out of their way as they went. They burst into the new establishment and parted a path towards the commotion. Two men circled each other with knives drawn. One man held a Bowie knife. He had a chest wound and the front of his shirt was drenched in blood. The other man carried a smaller spear knife. Blood ran down the side of his head where his ear had been, and a stomach wound left a trail of red clear to the crotch of his pants. Sheer willpower seemed to be the only thing keeping both men standing. A whore stood trapped from escape in a corner of the building.

Gideon and Finnie drew their revolvers.

"Drop your knives. You both need to see the doctor before you bleed to death," Gideon yelled.

The man with the missing ear staggered towards Gideon with his knife pointed towards the sheriff's stomach. His pace was unsteady and slow. Gideon slammed the barrel of the Colt down on the assailant's wrist, sending the knife clanking to the floor. Before the man could scream in pain, Gideon backhanded the barrel upside the attacker's head, sending him crashing to the floor.

In the commotion, the other man grabbed the whore and now held the Bowie knife to her neck. She screamed hysterically and a small trickle of blood ran from a knife nick.

"Let her go. You can't run. If you don't get to the doctor you'll die," Gideon shouted over the top of the whore's shrieks.

"Woman, if you don't shut the hell up I'm going to slit your throat just to quiet you," the man yelled in agitation.

The threat only made the woman more frantic. Unnerved and desperate, the wounded man appeared ready to make good on his promise. Gideon raised his gun and fired. The shot hit the hostage-taker above the bridge of his nose, sending him catapulting into the corner before sliding to the floor. The whore fainted and dropped on top of her assailant.

Finnie ran to the woman and dragged her off the man before examining her neck.

"How bad is it?" Gideon asked.

"I've cut myself worse shaving," Finnie answered.

Cyrus Capello walked out from behind the bar. "Sheriff, I can always get another whore, but I can't get more patrons if we develop a reputation for killing them off. You seem to be a bit hasty with your gun," he chided.

"Shut up or you'll be on the floor with the rest of them," Gideon warned. He holstered his gun to ward off the urge to club the saloon owner.

Finnie picked up the whore and headed for the door.

"What happened to start all this?" Gideon asked.

A man standing nearby said, "They got into an argument over the whore and pulled their knives and went to work on each other."

"Does anybody know these two?"

Nobody seemed to know either man.

"Some of you carry this man to Doc," Gideon said, pointing to the one he had waylaid. "Some others take that one to the undertaker."

By the time Gideon walked into the doctor's office, Doc had the whore's neck bandaged and had revived her with smelling salts. She remained hysterical and the doctored plied her with brandy to calm her nerves. Before Gideon could ask of her condition, the patrons of the bar carried the injured man in and flopped him on the table. The whore let out another scream and Finnie grabbed the bottle of brandy before leading the woman over to the doctor's desk.

As Doc ripped the injured man's shirt open, the man opened his eyes and moaned. He looked straight up at the ceiling with a glazed stare. The knife wound ran from the bottom of his sternum past his belly button. Doc washed his hands and poured carbolic acid over them before sticking his fingers into the wound and running them the length of the injury. Gideon watched as the doctor's fingers completely disappeared inside of the man.

Doc pulled his hand out and wiped away the blood on a towel. "I'd have a better chance of putting one of Sheriff Fuller's fish back together after he cleaned it than I do of repairing this man. He's completely disemboweled," he said.

"What's your name?" Gideon asked.

The man blinked his eyes a couple of times before closing them. He took a few more breaths before his chest went still.

"Welcome to the grand opening of the Pearl West Saloon," Gideon muttered.

Chapter 6

Zack had sat on the back of his horse for nine days running. He'd kept track of the time, but he could feel that today was Sunday without having to think. After a childhood of his aunt and father taking him to church every week, he could sense the Sabbath. He thought the day had serenity to it like no other and also a loneliness if you were by yourself and a long way from home.

The travel had been easy after traipsing through the mountains to arrive at the plains. He'd wasted little time, only stopping occasionally in a town for a hot meal. Denver had been a bit of a disappointment. He wasn't sure what he had been expecting, but whatever it was, he didn't find it. After riding through Fort Collins, the land gradually changed into foothills. He figured he had to be getting close to the Wyoming Territory border and would make Laramie sometime on Monday.

Around noontime, Zack spotted what looked to be a man walking a horse farther up the trail going the same direction that he traveled. As he neared them, he could see that the animal was a big mule with no saddle and only a rope around the neck to lead the beast. He rode up on them undetected.

"Are you all right?" Zack called out.

The man jumped as if shot, and spun around. "Sweet Jesus, you scared me. I mean no one harm," he said with a southern accent.

Zack looked the man over. The traveler appeared to be about thirty years old and poor. His clothes were worn out and his hat had lost all semblance of shape. He stood small in stature and looked as if he could use a good feeding.

"Me likewise. My name is Zack Barlow. Have you had some trouble?" Zack asked as he climbed down off his horse and offered his hand.

The man vigorously pumped Zack's hand. "I'm Justin Warf. My wagon is about a mile up the trail with my wife and two children. A couple of men robbed us this morning and scattered my two mules. They took everything valuable we had, but I consider us lucky that we're still alive and my wife not taken advantage of. I caught Cleo, but Sissy won't let me near her. That's her over yonder. She likes to keep me in sight, but at arm's length so to speak," Justin said.

"I'll catch her for you. Where are you from?" Zack inquired.

"Thank you, sir. We're from Tennessee. My brother runs a mill in Laramie. He wrote me to come work for him. I'm just a sharecropper and figured we could make a better life out here. Those men stole a hundred and fifty dollars from us. Do you know how long it takes to save that kind of money sharecropping? They got my watch, rifle, shotgun, and my wife's brooch too."

"Is Thomas Warf your brother?"

Justin's face betrayed surprise. "He is. Do you know him?"

"I'm from Laramie originally and met him a couple of times. Nice enough fellow," Zack answered.

"Small world I guess."

"Let me catch your mule and then I'll ride back to your wagon with you."

Back when Zack moved to Colorado and had gone to work on Ethan's ranch, he was more likely to lasso himself than his target, but with his boss's guidance, he had become a pretty fair roper. He trotted out towards the mule, preparing his rope as he rode. Sissy took off as he neared and Zack heeled his horse in pursuit. He let the rope fly and watched as the lasso settled onto the animal's neck. With a tug, the mule came to a stop and then followed him back to her owner.

"Much obliged. I'm not sure I'd have ever caught that hardheaded mule," Justin said.

Zack rode to the wagon with Sissy in tow while Justin walked with the other mule. They found Justin's wife sitting by the fire with her two children huddled against her. She was sobbing with worry over Justin's absence all morning and remained distraught about the robbery.

"This is my wife Claire and that is Davey and Annie," Justin said as an introduction.

Zack nodded his head at the family while Claire gathered herself.

After helping hitch the team, Zack said, "I'm going to try to get your things back. Head on towards Laramie. I'll catch up with you somewhere on the trail or in town whether I get your things back or not. If you don't see me again, please notify my Aunt Sharon Barlow in Laramie and tell her what happened."

"Sir, you don't have to do that. My brother can put us up until we get back on our feet. There's no need for you getting yourself killed over our misfortune," Justin warned.

"I've been in your shoes and somebody helped me. Now is my time to repay the debt. And I don't plan on getting killed," Zack said before mounting his horse. He tipped his hat before locating the outlaws' tracks and riding away.

The robbers had headed north. Zack figured they planned to ride past a mountain range and then heads towards Cheyenne. The knowledge that he'd be riding away from Laramie put a damper on his spirit. He wanted to see his aunt before trying to woo Joann back home. Now all that would have to wait. Just the thought of riding towards where Joann lived quickened his heartbeat and made him long for his wife.

A chill settled into the air in the afternoon and the wind kicked up a short time later. By the time dusk arrived, the sky spit snow. Zack had tracked the outlaws past the mountain range where they had turned and headed northeast in the direction of Cheyenne. He hoped that the men would make camp and not push on into the night to reach the town. Once they made Cheyenne, he feared he'd lose them for good.

As darkness fell, so did the temperature and the snow picked up a little. Zack stopped to bundle himself in his heavy coat and then resumed riding northeast. Thankfully, the cold front hadn't hid the stars by which he set his course. He figured he would either come upon a campfire or continue traveling until he hit Cheyenne. After a couple of hours of riding, he spotted a flicker of light in the distance. He kept riding until he judged he must be about a quarter of a mile from the campfire. After tying his horse in some brush, Zack started walking. He reached into his vest pocket and pulled out the badge that Gideon had given him to use whenever the sheriff needed an extra gun. Zack smiled as he recalled teasing Gideon that the lawman only needed him when there was a chance to get his son-in-law killed. He pinned the badge onto his coat knowing he had no jurisdiction, but hoped it might still give the outlaws pause. As he got closer, he could see the two men huddled around the fire and hear their voices. He stood in the darkness and waited what felt like forever before the men crawled into their bedrolls. The cold seemed to have sunk into his every pore and he shivered as he lingered until he felt sure the men slept.

By the time Zack reached the camp, the walking had his circulation going again and had warmed his limbs. The two men snored with their holsters resting by their sides. Zack walked over, retrieved the two gun belts, and tossed them to the side. As he pulled out his revolver, he reared his leg back and kicked the nearest outlaw in the hip. The man shot upright off the ground, yelping as he did so, and reaching for his now missing gun. Startled, the second outlaw did the same.

Zack cocked his Colt. "You boys shouldn't go robbing a poor family. I have you about as helpless as you did those people. Now give me the things you took or I'll kill you and find it myself," he said.

Wincing with pain and rubbing his hip, the kicked man said, "You can't just shoot us without provocation."

"Big word for someone that makes his living by stealing, but you mistake me for someone that gives a damn about the intricacies of the law. Is that a big enough word for you?" Zack asked.

"Wally, give him the money and things. We made a poor choice on this one," the second man said.

Wally, still aching from the kick, got to his feet and limped to a saddlebag where he retrieved a wad of cash along with a watch and brooch. "Those guns there belong to the southerner," he said.

"Set their things down and back up," Zack ordered.

After placing the money and jewelry on the ground, Wally lingered. "You're a big talker with a gun in your hand, but I'm not so sure you aren't robbing us just like we did those folks. We may cross paths again someday."

Wally had begun to grate on Zack's nerves. The outlaw seemed awfully boisterous for a cornered thief. Zack felt a slow rage building. He wasn't sure if he really hated Wally that much or if the robber just made for a convenient scapegoat for all that had gone wrong in his life lately. Holstering his revolver, Zack sent a right hook into Wally's jaw. As the outlaw's knees buckled, Zack pummeled him to the ground.

Zack had been as inept at fighting as he was at lassoing when he arrived in Last Stand. Finnie had been trained as a boxer and had taught him the art of fisticuffs. Plopping down on Wally's stomach, Zack began battering the man's face. Each punch he delivered felt as if it were a blow to all the injustice that life had dealt him and Joann. He was lost in his rage when the second man grabbed him from behind and wrapped an arm around his neck. Zack felt the outlaw reaching to try to steal his gun. He threw his elbow back as hard as he could into the ribs of the man and heard them crack. The outlaw screamed into Zack's ear before falling away. Zack resumed punching Wally before jumping up to find the whereabouts of the second outlaw. He found him crawling towards the guns. Drawing his Colt, Zack then darted for the man and crashed the barrel across the back of the outlaw's skull. The man dropped as if dead. As Zack spun around, he saw Wally on all fours attempting to get to his feet. Zack took two steps and kicked the robber in the face as hard as he could. Wally landed on his back and did not move.

Standing there, Zack let his rage fade away as he caught his breath. He gathered up the outlaw's guns and walked into the darkness, tossing them. He then shoved the family's belongings into the pocket of his coat and picked up the southerner's two guns. After untying the thieves' two horses, he led them away and began the walk towards where he had left his mount.

Zack's heartbeat returned to normal and he calmed down enough to notice that the snowfall had picked up so that it was beginning to stick to the ground. He took in a big breath and exhaled slowly. Over the years he'd been in some close spots, and even been shot once, but never had he attempted something as daring as what he had just done. Troubled by his carelessness, he wondered what had come over his usual placid nature.

His horse nickered, forcing Zack out of his reverie as he searched for and found the gelding. He mounted up and began riding with the outlaw's two horses in tow. After covering a couple of miles, he stopped to remove the leads from the animals. He gave the horses a good slap on the ass and the animals bolted. The outlaws would have the pleasure of retrieving their mounts just as they had done to the southerner. Zack looked around the best that he could in the dark, but finding little in the way of cover from the snow, he decided to ride through the night. To his way of thinking, it'd be better to keep moving than lie on the cold ground and shiver as the snow drifted up against the blankets.

He tried to keep on a straight course to the west. The snow pelted him out of the northwest, but he managed to do a pretty fair job of staying on track by paying attention to how the snow smacked him in the face. Occasionally the snow would stop and the sky would clear long enough that he could get his bearings from the stars.

Feeling numb all over, Zack wondered if he were frozen to the saddle. Snow continuously stuck to his eyelashes and he attempted to swipe the moisture away with the sleeve of his coat. Gideon's advice to take the train kept going through his head and forced him to smile as he realized that age and experience sometimes trumped youthful exuberance.

After what seemed like an eternity, the sky began to lighten to gray behind him. By the time the sun had risen above the horizon, the snow had stopped and the morning looked as clear as a bell. Zack came upon the trail that headed north to Laramie and spotted the wagon up ahead. He put his horse into a lope and found the family huddled around a fire as the wife cooked breakfast.

"Y'all made it back," Justin drawled.

"I did and I have your money and belongings," Zack said as he pulled off his gloves and retrieved the money, watch, and brooch.

Claire threw her hands to her face before saying, "Bless you. You're like an angel sent to us."

Zack smiled. "I don't think anybody has ever called me that before."

"Well, you are to us," Claire said.

Justin noticed the bruises and raw knuckles on Zack's hands. "Looks like you had trouble," he said and nodded towards the injuries.

"That was my own fault. I got careless. Everything came out just fine."

"Breakfast is just about ready. At least we have plenty of food," Claire announced as she poured Zack a cup of coffee.

The coffee tasted as good as any Zack could remember. It and the fire warmed him until he could feel his toes again.

As they ate breakfast, Claire asked Zack about himself. He had grown comfortable with the family and told them about Joann, Tess, and the reasons for his travel. After finishing the meal, the wife disappeared into the back of the wagon. She emerged a few minutes later with a slip of paper.

"I wish we had something to give you as a reward. I wrote you out this bible verse and I want you to carry it in your pocket. We'll be praying for you and your wife every night. On that you have my word. I want you to do the same," Claire said as she handed Zack the note.

Zack looked at the paper and read aloud, "Do not be anxious about anything, but in everything by prayer and supplication with thanksgiving let your requests be made known to God."

The verse flooded him with emotion. His hands trembled almost imperceptibly as he held the note and goosebumps popped up on his arms. Claire's thoughtfulness had not only given him hope, but also made him feel a spiritual connection that he hadn't felt in a very long time. He steeled himself from getting teary eyed. "Thank you," was all that he managed to say as he looked Claire in the eye.

Claire reached over and patted Zack's leg. "I have a good feeling about Joann. You're a good man. God be with you," she said.

Carefully folding the paper, Zack placed the verse in his pocket. He smiled at Claire and shook Justin's hand. "I'm heading on into Laramie. You should easily make it there today. I'm glad we crossed paths and I certainly won't forget any of you," he said before walking to his horse.

Zack gave a little wave and the family waved back until he rode out of sight.

Chapter 7

Abby sat down at the breakfast table all smiles and humming. She planned to interview two men for the position of a full-time ranch hand that morning. During the fall, Gideon and she had cleaned and repaired an old outpost shack that resided on some property they had purchased on auction after the death of the rancher, Frank DeVille. The one room cabin looked like nothing to write home about, but they had transformed the place into suitable quarters for a cowboy.

"You're in a fine mood this morning," Gideon noted as Abby passed him the biscuits.

"I am. I plan to hire one of those two men today. Now that we've expanded the herd, we need someone in place before winter arrives," Abby said.

"Well, I wouldn't get my hopes up too strongly. There's a reason that neither one of those two are employed right now. Charlie is known to not follow orders and Roger is a fall down drunk," Gideon reminded his wife.

"You certainly are taking a dim view on the matter," Abby said, giving Gideon a stern look.

"This idea of growing the herd is all yours and yours to see to. You know I've had misgivings about it from the get go. I still think we should've found a good ranch hand before we bought all those heifers. Look at poor Ethan. With Zack gone, he's had to hire Fuzzy Clark, and Fuzzy isn't any better than the two you're thinking about hiring."

"That's a bit of an indifferent attitude to take," Abby said as she helped Chance with his meal.

"I'm not indifferent at all when it comes to our money, but I told you that I have my hands full being sheriff. I'd think you'd be thrilled that I trust my wife enough to go along with this plan."

Abby grinned at her husband. "Gideon Johann, you are a smooth talker. Throwing me a compliment as you're telling me that this is all my responsibility is a nice bit of politicking. No wonder they elected you sheriff."

Gideon tore off a piece of bacon with his teeth and grinned. "You're just easy. I could always charm the pants . . . uh, I could always charm you," he said as he noticed Winnie intently following the conversation.

"So you say. So you say. I think I'll put you to the test tonight," Abby said and winked.

"So you say. I have to go. Breakfast tasted good as usual," Gideon said as he stood. He leaned over and kissed each of the children before turning towards Abby. Using his body to shield Winnie's view, he gave his wife a kiss that he hoped would keep him on her mind all day.

After Gideon left, Abby let the children play and gave Winnie instructions on taking her little brother outside when the company arrived. On the occasions when she needed a babysitter for Chance, Abby really missed Joann. Her daughter would have gladly come over and watched her younger siblings if she still lived here. Abby had thought about taking Winnie and Chance over for Ethan's wife Sarah to watch, but feared that it wouldn't look proper to interview the ranch hands with no one else home.

An hour later, Charlie Hibbs arrived on time. Red began barking to alert the family of his arrival and Abby shooed the children outside as she walked onto the porch.

"Good morning, Mr. Hibbs. Won't you come inside," Abby greeted as the man climbed off his horse.

"Morning, ma'am," Charlie said as he looked towards the barn. "Is Gideon here?"

"No, he went to town. I'll be talking to you about the job, Mr. Hibbs."

"But Gideon is the one that asked me to come out here about the job."

"Yes, he did that on my behalf," Abby said before disappearing into the cabin.

Following her inside, Charlie took off his hat and waited until Abby motioned for him to take a seat.

"Mr. Hibbs, I'm looking to hire someone that is capable of tending to the cattle on his own with direction from me," Abby stated.

"No offense, ma'am, but don't you think you'd be best at tending to the young ones. Ranching is a man's calling. I'm used to taking orders from an experienced foreman," Charlie said.

"My qualifications are not of your concern, Mr. Hibbs. You need only trouble yourself with tending to the herd and following orders," Abby said testily.

"I reckon I'm not suited for taking orders from a woman. That's not the natural order of things, ma'am."

"Thank you for your time. I think we are done here," Abby said as she stood and waited for the ranch hand to leave. Charlie wasted no time in heading for the door.

After Charlie left, Abby walked outside to check on Winnie and Chance. She felt so mad that she thought she might pop a button. Chance walked over to his mother and wrapped his arms around her leg. He looked up at her with his beaming smile.

Smiling back, Abby said, "Yes, Chance, there are more important things in this world than getting mad at some old ranch hand."

Abby sat down on the steps and put Chance in her lap while Winnie sat down and scooted up next to her mother.

"Is that man going to work for us?" Winnie asked.

"No, I'm afraid not. He doesn't want to be bossed around by a woman. He thinks we should all stay at home and have babies and make apple pie," Abby answered.

"He made you mad, didn't he?"

"Yes, a little bit. Winnie, things are changing. A girl can go out and do whatever she wants to in life. If she wants to stay home and have babies, well, that's fine. And if she wants to run a ranch or own her own store, well, that's fine, too. Look at how well Mary runs the saloon. I'd challenge any man to run the Last Chance better than she does," Abby said, her words picking up steam as she went.

"Maybe I'll run a ranch and Benjamin can work for me," Winnie said.

Benjamin Oakes was the son of Ethan and Sarah. The two children were of the same age. They had known each other since they were babies and held a mutual fascination with one another. Some adults speculated that the two were destined to spend their lives together while others felt the children would come to develop a sibling relationship as they matured.

Abby let out a giggle. "I have a feeling that poor old Benjamin will be working for you one way or the other."

The family remained sitting on the porch until Roger Sams rode into the yard. Abby sent the children to play as Roger climbed down from his horse and began walking to the cabin. Staggering ever so slightly as he walked, Abby realized that the ranch hand had been drinking.

"Have you been drinking before noon?" Abby asked as she stood before the cowboy.

Surprised by her boldness, Roger pulled his head back and peered down at Abby. "Just a little to knock off the chill. It was mighty cool this morning," he said.

The smell of whiskey hit Abby with near nauseating force. "Mr. Sams, get back on your horse and get out of here. I won't tolerate such behavior. Now go," she barked out.

Abby watched the drunkard ride off as she sat back down on the step. Her previous good mood had faded like a sunset. She had the urge to cry, but wouldn't allow herself the emotion in front of the children. Gideon had been right in his assessment of the two men, but she refused to believe she had bit off more than she could chew. She straightened her posture and pulled her shoulders back, determined not fail.

∞

In the early afternoon, a woman had showed up at the jail complaining that her neighbor's goats had eaten her sheets off the line. She warned that she was about to do some killing if the law didn't handle things. Gideon gladly sent Finnie to settle the dispute. The

Irishman gave him a look that could have killed, but Gideon didn't care. All day long, Finnie had been even more loquacious than usual and he was about on the sheriff's last nerve.

With Finnie out of the way, Gideon decided to go have a talk with the deputy's wife. Since Mary had had the baby, she didn't have the time to sit around and talk with Gideon like the old days, and he missed their conversations. In fact, he considered his chats with Mary necessary to keep himself grounded. As he walked towards the saloon, he smiled and wondered what it said about himself that he was married to a feisty, opinionated woman, and that two of his best friends, Mary and Sarah, both wouldn't think twice on setting him straight if need be.

He walked into the saloon and sat down at his usual table. The lunch crowd had thinned out and only a couple of regulars stood at the bar. Delta saw him come in and went to the back room. Mary returned with the barmaid, poured a beer, and sat down with Gideon.

"What brings you back so soon? Didn't our lunch satisfy you?" Mary asked as she pushed the beer towards Gideon.

"I sent your husband on an errand and I thought I'd use the time to have an intelligent conversation. He's wound tighter than a clock today and has about talked my ears off with his blathering," Gideon said before sipping the beer.

"There you go again talking badly about my husband," Mary said playfully.

"Most times you agree with me," Gideon said and smiled.

"He's been on his best behavior lately and he does more than his fair share on helping with Sam."

"I miss our talks. How are you doing?"

"Life is pretty darn good. I'm tired most the time, but happy. I'll be glad when I get that child off the breast. I tell you he's a little glutton. That little sawed-off deputy makes a pretty good husband and I sure never thought I'd ever be raising a child," she said.

"Life's funny for sure. We both know that."

"And how about yourself?" Mary asked.

"Good. Winnie and Chance are doing well. Chance is learning new things all the time. That's a fun age. We got a telegram from Zack today and he made it to his Aunt Sharon's place. I worry about him and Joann, but I guess time will take care of that."

"How is Abby? I haven't gotten to see her and Sarah as much lately. I miss our girl chats."

"Abby was supposed to talk to Charlie Hibbs and Roger Sams about coming to work for us today. I warned her about both of them. I don't imagine things went so well."

"Oh, my goodness, both of those would be a mistake."

"I know. I told her when she came up with this idea to expand the ranch that it was all on her. She'll have to figure it out."

"Gideon, don't you think you should be helping her?"

"No, she needs to do this on her own. She needs a challenge and to prove to herself that she's capable. I know that she'll figure things out and be better for it."

Mary smiled. "Well, aren't you the sage? I know somebody that you could try to hire. String Callow is always complaining that he'll never make foreman as long as he works at the Harris Ranch. He's a bit of a loner and I think he'd do well on his own as long as Abby didn't rein him in too tightly. You might have to pay him a little extra to get him away, but I've heard what a good hand he is."

Gideon rubbed his scar and grinned. "That business woman brain of yours is always thinking. How do you propose we make a gesture towards String without looking as if we are poaching him from Harris?"

"Let me take care of that. I'll see String in here and find out if he wants to talk to Abby. I can be persuasive, you know?" Mary said and brashly bobbed her head.

"I'd never doubt a woman that sobered up a little Irish drunk and turned him into a family man," Gideon said and gave her a wink. "For the record, we never had this conversation. After all, Abby is doing this and not me."

Chapter 8

Making a mid-morning walk of the town, Gideon thought that everything seemed back to normal the Wednesday after the hanging. All of the out-of-towners were long departed and the carpenters had removed all signs of the gallows as if it had never existed. Three fresh graves occupied the cemetery – two of them unmarked. And thankfully, the jail remained free of prisoners for the first time in a good while.

As Gideon walked in front of the Pearl West, out stepped the barker that had bellowed out the grand opening of the saloon as Kurt Tanner still swung in the wind.

In a voice soft and calm, the barker said, "Mr. Capello would like a moment of your time, if you please."

Gideon didn't answer but followed the employee into the saloon where he was led to an office off to the side of the bar. Cyrus Capello sat behind an impressive walnut desk with brass trim. The barker quickly took his leave.

"Good morning, Sheriff," Cyrus said. "Won't you have a seat?"

Sitting down in one of the two padded leather chairs facing the desk, Gideon waited for the saloonkeeper to speak.

Cyrus pulled out a bottle of whiskey from a drawer along with two shot glasses. "Care for a drink?" he asked.

"Little too early in the morning for my taste," Gideon said.

"It's never too early for fine whiskey. It cleans out the pipes," Cyrus said and poured himself a shot that he drank down in one gulp.

"What can I do for you? I have better things to do than sit and watch you drink," Gideon said with a hint of annoyance.

"Yes. Yes, I'm sure you do," Cyrus said as he eyed the sheriff as if taking stock of him. "I wanted to apologize for my outburst the other night when you had to shoot the drunkard. You had a duty to rescue that whore and I should've kept quiet."

Gideon nodded his head and studied Cyrus, trying to figure out the saloon owner's endgame.

"You have to understand my point of view, too. Too much law is bad for saloon business. I hope you can minimize interfering with the natural state of my operation."

Rubbing his scar, Gideon looked around the room before speaking. "In other words, you're sorry, but I best not do that again."

Cyrus flashed a toothy grin. "You're a smart man, Sheriff. I'm sure we'll both come to appreciate the mutual benefits of cooperation between the two of us."

"I don't know about smart. In fact, I believe I would argue against the point, but I am hardheaded and I sure as hell can't be intimidated. Your cooperation and not mine will be required for a happy coexistence," Gideon said as he arose from the chair and headed out the door without bothering to see Cyrus's reaction.

Walking across the street and into the jail, Gideon slammed the door as he entered. Finnie, trimming his fingernails with a penknife, nearly jumped out of his chair.

"Damn, you nearly caused me to cut off a finger," the Irishman protested.

"Sorry, Cyrus Capello just had me in for a little meeting. That man is going to be nothing but trouble. I'd like to knock the teeth out of that toothy grin of his," Gideon said as he dropped into his chair and tossed his hat.

"I told you as much. There's a reason he's been run out of every other town before we had the pleasure of making his acquaintance," Finnie said as he resumed trimming his nails.

"I know you did. He has another thing coming if he thinks he's going to run this town. Cyrus can try to buy off the whole town, but he will follow the law."

Mayor Hiram Howard walked into the jail. "Have you heard the news?" he asked.

Hiram was an affable enough man and Gideon liked him even though he considered the mayor a bit on the excitable side.

"Heard what?" Gideon asked.

"They say a Mexican from California and his crew brought twenty-thousand sheep into the county yesterday. The word is that sheep are so thick in California that you can't shoot a gun without hitting one. The prices have bottomed out and they're running out of room to graze the wooly beasts," Hiram said excitedly.

Gideon sucked in a gulp of air and puffed up his cheeks as he exhaled slowly. "I sure hope you're wrong. These ranchers were agitated enough with those four brothers coming here. If the cattlemen think they are about to be overran with sheep, they will get irrational and nasty."

"I believe my source to be true. I need to get back to the store, but I thought you should know," Hiram said before departing.

Finnie folded his knife and stuck it into his pocket. "Remind me again why we chose to wear a badge," he said.

"It gives all our enemies something to aim at," Gideon said as he leaned back in his chair and put his hands behind his head.

"Well, in that case, I'm glad yours is bigger than mine – badge that is," Finnie said wryly.

Gideon let out a chortle. "So you say. So you say," he said.

∞

Word quickly spread amongst the ranchers of the arrival of the huge flock from California. Lewis Wise rode over to Carter Mason's spread and found the rancher helping his cowboys repair the bunkhouse. Carter climbed down off the roof and walked over to the other rancher.

"What brings you out, Lewis?" Carter asked.

Lewis gave Carter the big news and then added, "I thought you and I might take a ride and see things for ourselves."

"Let's do it. Gives me an excuse to get out of helping the boys," Carter said as he twisted the end of his mustache.

The two men headed to where the flock was rumored to be grazing. Approaching the location from a high ridge overlooking the valley, they spotted sheep below them for as far as the eye could see. Men on foot with dogs were cutting the flock into smaller groups and riders with rifles resting across their saddles rode the perimeter.

"Would you look at that? I can smell the stench from here. They even have guards. What self-respecting white man would work for a Mexican?" Lewis asked.

"I don't know, but that's a formidable operation," Carter said. The shock of the sight caused the rancher to twist both sides of his mustache at the same time.

"Yes, it is. We're going to have to make a statement in a roundabout way. Somebody could get killed if we approach this bunch."

"What are you thinking?"

"We'll get us up some men and stampede the flock of those four foreign brothers. We'll have pretty good moonlight tonight. Maybe when word gets out on what we think of sheep taking over our land, that Mexican down there will decide to keep right on moving," Lewis said as he turned his horse and headed back down the ridge.

Lewis and Carter recruited four other ranchers to help with the raid. They decided not to use ranch hands for fear one of them would get trigger-happy and to insure that no one bragged about their deeds. The six men met at Lewis's ranch well after dark. Lewis passed out a gunnysack to each man and waited as the ranchers cut eyeholes into the material.

"Here's what I'm thinking," Lewis began. "Me, Carter, and Andrew will try to cut out a quarter of the flock or so and run them towards Ute Cliff. We'll do us a little rim-rocking. You three scatter the rest of those damn sheep to kingdom come. There's no call to wipe out the whole flock. I don't bear those brothers that much ill will. I just want all the damn sheep out of our county."

The ranchers rode to where the four brothers were known to be grazing. On arriving, they found two flocks that Lewis figured made up half of the total sheep. The herding dogs had already started raising a ruckus.

"You boys scatter the flock to the west. We'll take the ones to the east. I guess those four brothers are each keeping an eye on a separate flock. Piss on the rest of them. We don't have all night to find the other two," Lewis said before kicking his horse into a lope.

The ranchers began yelling and firing their pistols as they descended on the flocks. The sheep panicked and began running in all directions, colliding into each other and piling together. One of the sheepherders ran out of his tent towards Lewis. He waved his arms wildly as if he hoped to flag the rancher down. Lewis saw the man at the last second and yanked hard on his reins to stop his horse, but the action came too late. The horse collided into the sheepherder with a disturbing thud, sending the sheepherder catapulting through the air and backflipping as he hit the ground.

"Damn it to hell," Lewis yelled as he reined his horse away.

Lewis, Carter, and Andrew began driving the flock towards the cliff a quarter of a mile away. Once they had the sheep going all in the same direction, the ranchers had little trouble guiding the animals where they wanted. The sheep ran over the cliff like ducklings hopping into a pond and disappeared from sight. Afterward, the three men walked to the edge and looked down. Darkness prevented a clear picture of what lay below, but a mound of white wool seemed to glow from the depths beyond and the bleating of injured animals echoed up the wall. Nobody spoke as the weight of their actions began to take hold.

To end the silence, Lewis said, "Let's go meet the others back at that cottonwood we agreed upon. We all need to be getting home."

Dominique Laxalt and his brother, Ander, were tending to the two flocks that the ranchers never located. They had both taken off running towards the sound of the gunfire. By the time they reached the spot where the other flocks had been bedded down, the ranchers were long gone. They stood there sucking in air trying to catch their breaths and calling out their brothers' names. Peru Laxalt answered their calls. Crying and disoriented, he came walking up to his brothers.

"Where is Julen?" Dominique asked in his Euskera language.

"I don't know. I can't find him and he won't answer," Peru answered.

The three brothers began searching for Julen. They trampled around in the dark for over an hour before Ander came upon his brother. Julen lay unconscious and unresponsive to his brother's pleas to open his eyes. As Dominique and Peru ran to assist, Ander found Julen's pulse and leaned close to listen to his brother's breathing.

"He's alive and breathing," Ander called out.

"We need to take him to the doctor. I'll hitch the wagon while you two stay with him. Try to make him comfortable and see if he'll take some water," Dominique said before disappearing into the dark.

Shortly thereafter, Dominique returned on the wagon. The three brothers gently lifted Julen into the buckboard and placed him on a pallet of blankets.

"Ander, stay here with the sheep. Peru can care for Julen as I drive to town," Dominique said as he handed his brother one of the two shotguns they owned. "Be careful and hide if they return. We need you."

Nodding his head, Ander climbed down from the wagon and watched the buckboard head into the darkness.

Dominique and his brothers arrived in Last Stand well after midnight. He stopped the wagon in the middle of the street with the sheriff and doctor's offices on his either side. The town had shut down for the night and the street was empty of people. Not knowing where the doctor's office was located or how to read English, Dominique fired off the two loads in his shotgun, one at a time, and then started yelling for help.

Doc Abram nearly fell from his bed to the floor from startling so violently at the roar of the gun. He lay in his bed as his heart raced like a horse galloping and tried to get his senses about him. Realizing that somebody needed him, he threw on his robe and lit a lamp before walking to the door. Cautiously peeking out, he didn't recognize the men in the wagon.

"I'm the doctor. Can I help you?" Doc called out.

Dominique began rambling in Euskera before catching himself and switching to English. "My brother hurt bad. Won't wake," he said.

"Bring him in while I light some lamps," Doc said before disappearing back into his office.

The brothers carried Julen in and set him on the table that Doc stood beside. The doctor began examining Julen's head and found a goose egg knot on the back of the skull. Doc lit a small candle and pulled Julen's eyelid open as he moved the light towards the eye. The eye reacted to the light. He then turned the man's head and watched as the eye moved counter-wise. Grabbing a suture needle, Doc poked the sheepherder's arm and elicited no response.

"He's in a coma. He's hurt bad," Doc said.

"What coma?" Dominique asked.

"Deep sleep. He can't wake up," Doc answered.

The sheepherder translated to his brother as he pulled off his hat and wiped his forehead.

Doc returned to Julen and examined the rest of his body. "What happened?" he asked as he worked.

"Gunnysackers," Dominique said angrily and pounded the counter for emphasis before going on to explain what he knew.

After finishing the exam, Doc said, "I think his head is his only injury, but it could be serious. I'll know more in the morning."

"What we do?"

"He needs to stay here. Moving him would be bad and you need to see the sheriff in the morning. Sleep on my floor tonight," Doc said as he removed his spectacles.

"Thank you, Doctor," Dominique said. "We cause no trouble. Men won't let us be."

Chapter 9

As Gideon rode to the jail, he noticed the horse and wagon in front of the doctor's office. He thought he recognized the rig as the one that the sheepherder had used the day that there had been trouble in town. A sinking feeling settled over him and he let out a sigh as he climbed off Buck. After tying up his horse, he walked inside his office and had no more than sat down when Dominique, and what looked to be his brother, came into the jail.

"Men stampeded our flocks. My brother hurt bad," Dominique said as he walked up to the sheriff.

Gideon tossed his hat on the desk and ran both hands through his thatch of hair. He'd feared this day was coming and didn't have a clue on how a sheriff and one deputy could put a stop to the harassment. Rubbing his scar, he began questioning Dominique, who in turn translated the questions to his brother. By the time the interrogation ended, Gideon had only learned that the men wore gunnysacks. Peru had no idea how many men had been involved and couldn't describe a single horse or rider.

"Sit right here while I go talk to the doctor," Gideon said after giving up on finding out any useful information.

Doc sat at his desk drinking coffee when Gideon walked into the office. The doctor looked tired and as if he'd rather be in bed.

"How bad is the sheepherder?" Gideon asked.

"Bad. He's in a coma," Doc said as he rubbed his eye.

"Do you think he'll recover?"

"Hard to say. He could wake up this afternoon or he could stay that way until he starves to death or his brain could be swelling until it dies. His condition hasn't changed since they brought him in here."

"I'm going to have a mess on my hands if all these ranchers turn vigilante. How do you stop that?"

"You might have to bring in reinforcements. That's what a U.S. Marshal is for," Doc said.

"I'm not sure how much help I'd get trying to protect sheepherders. They might rank lower than Indians," Gideon mused. "I'll see you later."

Gideon found Finnie making coffee in the jail when he returned. Once the coffee cooked, the deputy poured four cups and handed one of them to each of the brothers.

Sipping from his cup, Gideon made a face. "Good God, Finnie, do you think you got it strong enough?" he asked.

"Oh, shut up. Nobody wants to hear a whiner first thing in the morning," Finnie retorted.

"If it were any stronger, I'd have to spoon it out."

"You're like the man that got the free poke at the whorehouse and went around complaining that all the girls were too well-used to fit properly until someone called attention to the fact that the size of the man might be the problem," Finnie said.

"All of your whorehouse analogies. Sometimes I don't even know what they mean and I doubt you do either."

Dominique watched the lawmen quarrel and wondered if fisticuffs were about to break out between the two.

"What's the real problem?" Finnie asked.

Gideon rubbed the back of his neck. "Just a bad feeling about all this I guess."

"We've been in worse scrapes," Finnie reminded him.

"That we have," Gideon said. "That we have."

As the lawmen carried on their conversation, the sheepherder realized that the two men were more like brothers than anything else. Their obvious loyalty to each other gave him some reassurance to his and his brothers' plight.

"Why ranchers hate us?" Dominique asked.

Gideon glanced over at Finnie, hoping the loquacious Irishman would answer the question, but found him looking back with an expression than plainly inferred that the inquiry was in the sheriff's domain.

"I guess lots of reasons. The ranchers were the ones that settled this part of the country and drove off the Indians. They think that gives them rights to all the open range and they don't like to share. Sometimes not even with each other. Lastly, they say that sheep ruin the land and foul the water," Gideon said.

Dominique nodded his head as if he agreed before saying, "But they don't own open range. Everybody's land. Sheep not hurt water. Won't hurt grass if not left there too long."

Gideon liked the way the sheepherder made eye contact when he talked. He felt empathy towards him and his brothers. They were no different from every other immigrant than had come to this country and tried to gain a share of its riches. "I'm not the one that you have to convince," Gideon said. "I'm going to ride out there and have a look. "What's your brother's name that you left behind?"

"Ander," Dominique answered. "Let me write him a note."

Draining his coffee cup, Gideon shuddered. "That's still the worst coffee you've ever made even going back to the war and that's saying something."

"You'll make it tomorrow come Hell or high water."

Gideon rode out and found the spot of the stampede. He called out Ander's name. The sheepherder appeared from behind some trees and walked to the sheriff. As Ander read the note from his brother, Gideon watched as the sheepherder pulled back his shoulders and inhaled a ragged breath to steel himself from the news. He motioned for the sheriff to follow him. Climbing down from his horse, Gideon walked with Ander to the cliff. What lay below the two men would have nauseated even someone that detested sheep. The animals were piled up in a pyramid that had to be fifteen feet high. Their bodies lay strewn in every position imaginable. A stench reached the two men from below and would surely become unbearable in a couple more days. Gideon motioned the best that he could that he planned to look around and then reached out to pat the sheepherder's shoulder.

Sheep stood around grazing everywhere that Gideon looked. The flocks had run in so many directions during the stampede that finding horse tracks proved impossible. Resigned to the fact that his efforts were useless, Gideon gave Ander a wave and rode away.

He headed for Lewis Wise's ranch. As Gideon tied his horse to a hitching post, he looked around the yard. The place appeared vacant until a ranch hand emerged from the barn walking a mare.

"Where is Lewis?" Gideon called out.

The ranch hand pointed towards the house. Gideon walked up to the entrance and banged the brass knocker. Lewis Wise opened the door almost immediately.

"Sheriff, what brings you out here?" Lewis asked.

"Can we talk out on the veranda?" Gideon asked.

"Sure," Lewis said as he stepped out and closed the door.

Lewis appeared as if he had just awakened. His face looked puffy and his eyes bloodshot. Gideon wondered if the rancher had lost sleep over a guilty conscience over the sheepherder's injuries.

"Somebody stampeded those four brothers' flocks and ran some of them off Ute Cliff. One of the brothers is badly hurt. In fact, he may die. You wouldn't happen to know anything about that, would you?" Gideon asked.

"No, I stayed here all night. You can ask my wife or any of the ranch hands for that matter."

"Lewis, those men are just trying to make a living like all the rest of us. Your word would go a long ways in getting folks to accept them and let them be."

"I don't bear any personal ill will towards those men, but you forget that they are a threat to our herds. You've seen what sheep do to grass. That land might as well be desert when they are done with it until the next spring."

Gideon studied the rancher's face searching for clues on whether Lewis told the truth. He wished Mary were here. She could spot a liar at fifty paces and he had a hunch that Lewis had lied.

"This is going to get a lot more serious if that sheepherder dies. I won't turn my back on it," Gideon said. "I'll be seeing you."

"Gideon, I have nothing to fear," Lewis said as the sheriff walked away.

As Gideon climbed aboard Buck, he wondered exactly what Lewis intended for those words to mean. Feeling like he wanted to run, Gideon put the horse in a lope all the way back to town.

He stopped in front of the doctor's office and went inside to check the sheepherder's condition. The doctor stood listening to the chest of a child while its mother hovered near the table. While taking a seat at the doctor's desk, Gideon doodled on a piece of paper until Doc finished the examination and sent them on their way.

"Anything change?" Gideon asked as Doc stood over him waiting for his seat.

"His eyes are no longer reacting to light," Doc said as he sat down in his chair.

"What does that mean?"

"It means his brain is dying. He'll quit breathing and his heart will stop."

"Do the brothers know?"

"Not yet. I'm waiting for them to get back. Finnie is looking out for them and took them to the Last Chance for lunch. They should be back anytime now," Doc said.

"Doc, sometimes I hate this job. I think I should've been a rancher instead."

"Some of us are meant for a life of service. This town has always needed me just like it needs you. That's our cross to bear," Doc said as he tossed his spectacles onto the desk.

Chapter 10

Gideon, Finnie, and Doc stood with the three Laxalt brothers as they buried Julen. The sheepherders were a pathetic sight as their naturally stoic dispositions crumbled under the grief for their youngest brother. Peru and Ander hugged each other as they cried, looking as if each needed the support of the other to remain standing. Once the grave was filled with dirt, Dominique thanked the lawmen and the doctor before quickly ushering his brothers to the wagon where a new shotgun rested on the seat. From now on each of the brothers would be armed. The family had little time to linger as they needed to get back to their flocks. They still hadn't had an opportunity to recover all the sheep that had been driven to God knew where.

Dominique held up the gun for Gideon to see. "If we must die, we die fighting," he said as Peru coaxed the horse to move down the cemetery road.

"You know what's surprised me?" Finnie asked as they began walking from the graveyard back to town. "As I've walked around town, I've had several of the townsfolks come up to me expressing their displeasure with the ranchers. They may have a low opinion of sheep, but they don't believe there's any call to go killing the sheepherders. Seems like people are getting fed up with the ranchers acting like they control everything in sight."

"You can't blame them. The big ranchers have been heavy-handed as long as I've lived here," Doc said as he struggled to keep pace with the two younger men.

"The town may be fed up, but that doesn't help us any in putting an end to all this. I fear we will be burying more of those brothers, and I don't know how we watch over them all the time," Gideon said with resignation.

"I don't know why we don't just arrest those ranchers. They may think they outfoxed everyone, but their ranch hands were smart enough to figure out which of their bosses rode out that night and came back late. Those cowboys practically made a game of it sitting around the Last Chance figuring out which ranchers were in on the stampede. They came up with six of them," Finnie said.

"They can know who the ranchers were all day long, but it's still just hearsay. We don't have a lick of evidence," Gideon said.

"Slow down, you two. You'll be old someday too and appreciate not being left behind like some old stallion put out to pasture," Doc groused.

"Well, Doc, if it's any comfort to you, we've always thought of you as more of a gelding," Finnie teased.

"I'll show you a gelding next time I get ahold of you. You'll be talking like a little girl," Doc threatened.

"I sure hope that doctor you hire has better bedside manners than you do. You could hurt a man's feelings," Finnie said.

Doc looked at Gideon as if he were to blame for Finnie's behavior and shook his head.

"Don't you dare look at me that way. I have no choice but to work with him. You choose to spend time with Finnie," Gideon reminded the doctor.

"Yeah, I wouldn't be faced with the choice, if you hadn't chosen to bring him to Last Stand and make him your deputy. Both of you just leave me alone," Doc said as he parted company and ambled towards his office.

"What are we going to do if he hires a new doctor and makes himself scarce?" Finnie asked.

"Except for taking a trip to Boston, I would imagine we would see more of him than ever. He'd likely be in the jail more than he is now. You two would probably kill each other," Gideon said.

"I'm what keeps him young. He'd more than likely be senile by now if he didn't have me to spar with," Finnie said as he walked into the jail.

"Just so you know, I'm staying in town tonight. With it being Friday and payday for the cowboys, I thought I'd stick around and see what goes on at the Pearl West."

"That dago really got under your skin the other day when he called you into his office, didn't he?"

"He did. These ranchers might get the best of us, but I'll be damn if Cyrus Capello does."

Gideon's plan to stay in town Friday night had pleased Abby none too well. He'd told her that he'd try to make it home late that night, but made no promises.

Around lunchtime, dark ominous clouds moved in and snow began falling and blowing down the street. Gideon contemplated going on home, but decided that the ranch hands wouldn't let snow stop them from coming to town with a pocketful of money. He wanted to impress upon Cyrus Capello right from the start that the saloonkeeper would not have his way in Last Stand.

Late in the afternoon, Gideon told Finnie to go home. The blustery weather had slowed business in town to the point that the streets were nearly empty of people. He wanted to take a nap before his long night ahead and knew sleep would be near impossible with the chatty Irishman sitting in the jail with him. After Finnie departed, Gideon dropped onto the cot and covered himself with a well-worn blanket. He fell right to sleep and slept for an hour before waking with a start from dreaming about Tess. With a toss of the blanket onto the floor, he stood and began pacing the room. He hated dreaming about his deceased granddaughter. The episodes always left him feeling as empty as a hollowed out log and wondering if he'd ever get past her death. The room had grown cold and he added some wood to the stove before sitting down at his desk. He kept a bottle of whiskey hidden in his drawer and pulled it out, taking a long drink. The whiskey didn't wash the memory away, but did relax him a little. He couldn't help but feel responsible for Tess's death. Deep down, he still harbored feelings that the tragedy was retribution for his past mistakes.

Finnie returned at a little after six o'clock. He asked Gideon to go dine with him at Mary's restaurant. The sheriff gladly accepted, ready for some conversation to change his mood. Outside, the snow sifted down in fluffy flakes the size of silver dollars and the wind had stilled. The air smelled of smoke from all the fireplaces burning in town to ward off the chill. The two men walked briskly to the diner where Charlotte seated them.

"You all right?" Finnie asked, sensing Gideon's dark mood.

"Yeah, sure, I'm fine. I'd just like to be home tonight," Gideon answered.

"Go on home. Nothing that happens in the Pearl West tonight won't happen again some other night."

"I know, but I want Cyrus to know that I plan to be a thorn in his ass right from the get-go," Gideon said, attempting a weak smile.

"What are we going to do?"

"You can spend your evening in the Last Chance or go home. I won't need you. We wouldn't want Mr. Capello to think that it takes both of us to watch over him."

"We wouldn't want that," Finnie joked.

"No, we wouldn't. I want him to know that he's met his match."

Charlotte walked up to the table. "Do you two know what you want to order? I thought maybe you were going to sit here holding hands and looking into each other's eyes all night," she said.

"I've said it before, but by God, you're a mean one," Finnie said. "I hate to think what you'll be like when you're an old maid."

"Who says I'm going to be an old maid?"

"Cecil Hobbs might have been dumb enough to want to marry you, but I can't imagine that there'd be a second one that addlebrained."

"You better watch your food tonight," Charlotte threatened.

To get the conversation back on track, Gideon said, "I'll have a beefsteak and a potato."

"I'll have the same," Finnie chimed in.

After Charlotte walked way, Finnie leaned across the table and said, "I'm not sure if she really dislikes me or she just likes to rile me."

"Oh, I think it's safe to say that it's the latter. If she disliked you, your food would be inedible."

For the rest of the meal, the two men talked of their families. Finnie did most of the talking, providing endless anecdotes about Sam. By the time they finished eating, Gideon feared he'd be privy to the details of Sam's bowel movements.

As they readied to part, Gideon said, "I probably won't see you until morning. Have a good night."

"Are you sure you won't need me?"

"I got this," Gideon said and walked towards the jail.

After throwing some wood into the stove, Gideon pulled a deck of cards from his desk and played solitaire. He didn't want to think about anything and occupied his mind with the game. At eight o'clock, he pulled on his coat and walked to the Pearl West.

Cowboys, not willing to let some snow ruin their opportunity to blow their pay, packed the saloon. Gideon walked up to the bar and ordered a beer. The bartender pushed the drink toward the sheriff and told him the drink was on the house, but Gideon retrieved a coin from his pocket and placed it next to the glass. With his back to the bar, Gideon looked around the room. Two tables had poker games a going, three Faro tables were in action, and cowboys crowded around the craps table. Craps provided a new game to most of the ranch hands and they were still trying to get a handle on the protocols and many types of bets.

Back in Boulder, Gideon had been a deputy for Sheriff Howell. The sheriff had taken the young Gideon under his wing and dragged the deputy to all the town's saloons, teaching him the various games and how to spot a cheater.

Gideon sipped his beer slowly as he watched all the happenings. When he finished off the mug, he ordered a second drink and began meandering through the crowd. He watched each of the tables for a little bit before moving to the craps table. The cowboys standing around the game were loud with hoots and hollering every time one of them threw the dice. Gideon maneuvered so that he could watch the house's stickman. As he did so, he noticed the bartender slip into the back. Cyrus hurried out of his office and took a position behind the bar. Gideon could feel the saloon owner watching him intently. Busy with the game, the stickman remained oblivious to the sheriff. Gideon observed that the man always kept his ring and little fingers folded into his palm. He watched as the stickman would occasionally make the slightest roll of his fingers and hand as he passed the dice to the shooter. Sheriff Howell had pointed out the switching of the dice trick to Gideon long ago in Boulder. This stickman was the best Gideon had ever seen at the switch.

As the stickman picked up the dice, Gideon glided in behind him and gave the man a good pop on the wrist. Four dice bounced onto the table. Before the stickman could turn to see what happened, Gideon grabbed him by the collar and shoved his head down into the craps pit.

"I don't appreciate you stealing these cowboys' hard earned money. The house has enough of an advantage without resorting to cheating," Gideon bellowed out loud enough to get the attention of most of the patrons of the saloon.

Cyrus Capello came rushing over to the table. "What's the problem here?" he asked.

"I caught your man cheating," Gideon said.

"Cheating," Cyrus said as if surprised. "David you're fired. You know I don't tolerate that kind of thing."

The cowboys were riled up now and surrounding Cyrus, demanding their money back.

Turning to the boxman, Cyrus ordered that all the cowboys be refunded their chips. In a booming voice, he then called for a free round of drinks for everybody in the house.

Gideon bent down close to the stickman's ear. "David, if you aren't on the stagecoach tomorrow, I'm coming to look for you, and you'll be freezing your ass off in a cell until the judge arrives. Do I make myself clear?" he yelled.

David nodded his head and Gideon released him.

"Sheriff, may I have a word with you in my office?" Cyrus asked before turning and walking away.

Gideon followed Cyrus into the office and the saloonkeeper shut the door.

"Sheriff, what in the hell are you trying to do to me? Do you have any idea how much money you just cost me?" Cyrus yelled as he walked behind his desk.

"I'm not trying to do anything but insure the games are fair," Gideon answered.

"I just had to fire the best stickman I've ever had. You know as well as I do that there's not a clean game in any saloon in Colorado," Cyrus said and pounded a fist on his desk.

"There will be in my town."

"You're hell-bent on being a pain in my ass, aren't you?"

Gideon smirked at the saloon owner. "I'm just upholding the law."

"Maybe we can come to some kind of arrangement that would be mutually beneficial to the both of us," Cyrus said as he pulled a cigar from his breast pocket.

"Are you trying to bribe me?"

"You said bribe, not me.   I asked if there was something we could find that would be mutually beneficial," Cyrus said before biting off the cap of the cigar.

"Go to hell," Gideon said as he turned and flung the door open.

Gideon walked out into the saloon.   Free drinks and the refunds of lost chips had pacified the crowd to the point that laughter and merriment had replaced any ill feelings.   After maneuvering his way through the sea of cowboys, Gideon exited out the door into the cold night air.   He took a deep breath and filled his lungs.   He had a bad feeling that he would be putting up with Cyrus Capello for a long time.   The saloonkeeper seemed crooked enough to try anything and crafty enough to let one of his underlings take the fall.

Chapter 11

After reaching Laramie, Zack's spinster Aunt Sharon had been so happy to see her nephew that he had to beg her to allow him some sleep before he caught her up on all the news. The traveling through the night after encountering the robbers had left him so weary that he could barely keep his eyes open. He fell asleep as soon as he dropped into his old bed and awoke just before supper to join his aunt for the meal. She had already received a letter from him concerning Joann's return to Cheyenne and of his plans for a visit. His aunt anxiously asked Zack about the latest on Joann. With nothing new to divulge concerning his wife, he told her about his encounter with the robbers. Zack could see the pride his aunt took in his actions to help the family even as she reproached him the whole time he told the story.

In the days that followed, Zack came to realize that his aunt's cooking and her companionship served as a balm to his fragile state. He had grown up in the home, and sleeping in his old room brought back memories of the happy times that he, his dad, and his aunt had shared in the house. His mother had died when Zack was two and he couldn't remember her, but his aunt had done her best to fill the void. Her home needed some repairs and Zack spent the days replacing shingles and mending other things that had fallen into disrepair. The work kept his mind free from his troubles and he got to bask in the glory of his appreciative aunt.

Though Joann lived little more than a day's ride away, her nearness caused him to begin to lose his nerve to follow through with his plans to see her. Every night before retiring to bed, Zack would pull the verse he'd been given from his pocket. He had read the passage so many times that he recited it while barely looking at the words. "Do not be anxious about anything, but in everything by prayer and supplication with thanksgiving let your requests be made known to God," he would whisper. Afterwards, he would say a prayer, but he could never get back the glorious feeling he had experienced when he read the verse for the first time with the Warf family. Dropping into bed each night, he'd fall asleep less sure than the previous day about a reunion with his wife.

One night at the supper table, Aunt Sharon asked, "So when are you planning to head to Cheyenne?"

"I don't know yet. I figure me and you have some lost time to make up for first and I want to make sure I have everything fixed in the house before winter starts for real. You don't need snowdrifts in the kitchen," Zack answered.

"I wish I had had the opportunity to spend more time with Joann and to get to know her better, but she seems like a fine girl. Life has dealt her a blow that she wasn't prepared to handle. I'd think you would be getting anxious to get over there and see her."

"I am anxious, but I fear the reception I'll receive when I get there. Joann can be such a force of nature and I expect her fury will be turned on me."

Smiling at his word, she said, "I feel sorry for both of you. Joann certainly never planned for things to turn out this way, though I do think that girl has an irrational streak and could learn to listen to some elderly advice. I pray for the two of you every night."

"Aunt Sharon, do you believe that prayer really helps?"

Sharon took her hand and patted her hair bun as she thought of her answer. "I do, Zack. There would be no point in having faith if we didn't believe in prayer. And if we didn't have faith, we might as well be monkeys," she said, nodding her head with conviction.

Chapter 12

After Gideon decided he best go check on the Laxalt brothers and meet the Mexican sheepherder, he rode out of town in the direction where the sheepherders had last made camp. From their old camp, he followed the path of eaten down grass until he came upon the brothers' wagon. As he rode to the top of a ridge, he spotted Dominique down below with his sheep. Dogs started barking, prompting the sheepherder to pull his shotgun off his shoulder and hold the gun waist high until he recognized the sheriff.

"Sheriff, what bring you?" Dominique asked as Gideon rode up.

"I thought I'd check and see if you've had any more trouble," Gideon replied.

"No trouble, but we ready."

"How are you and your brothers doing?"

Dominique shrugged his shoulders. "Life goes on, I guess. Julen the baby. I feel responsible. We lost almost two thousand sheep."

"I'm truly sorry. Be careful. I don't know if this is over with yet or not."

"Do you know who killed Julen?" Dominique asked.

Shaking his head, Gideon said, "Not yet. I'm having a hard time finding out anything."

Nodding his head, Dominique said, "Thank you. You honorable man. Goodbye."

The rumors concerning the Mexican sheepherder were that his flocks grazed farther to the northeast. Gideon rode for what he figured to be about three miles before he came upon pasture that had been so eaten down that it looked as if a severe drought had taken place. The damage caused pause – the ranchers were not entirely wrong in their concerns. Nothing would grow on this land again until the next spring. As much as he understood the sheepherders' rights to open range, he could sympathize with the ranchers' hatred for sheep and their mark upon the countryside.

Gideon spotted a guard watching him on a hillside. The sheriff gave the man a wave and rode to him. The rider looked to be in his fifties and a seasoned fighter. A scar ran across the bridge of his nose past his mouth to his jawline and black specs on his face gave the impression that a black powder explosion had permanently tattooed him.

"I'm Sheriff Gideon Johann. I was hoping to meet your boss today," Gideon said.

"What's your business?" the guard asked in a croaky voice that suggested further battle wounds.

"I just told you that I'm the sheriff. That's business enough."

"I'll have to go see if Mr. Cortez will receive you."

"No, I'm not waiting around. Either take me to him or I'm leaving and you can explain to your boss why you screwed up his opportunity to get to meet the sheriff on a social visit," Gideon said and turned his head and spit.

The guard sat on his horse a moment as he tried to figure out what to do. "Follow me," he finally said.

They rode for a quarter of a mile through a swale, until they came to an opening where the land flattened out into a lush green meadow. A large tent had been pitched and a fire with a spit was roasting a lamb. The man that had led Gideon to the spot dismounted and stuck his head into the tent. A few moments later, a man flung the door flap open and emerged from inside. He wore a black waistcoat, a white shirt, and black pants with a stripe running down the leg. On his head, he donned a wide, flat brimmed black hat. A mustache and goatee completed his appearance. Gideon locked his jaw to keep himself from laughing at the charade. The sheepherder certainly dressed the part of a Mexican aristocrat even if he lived in a tent on public land. The Mexican walked straight to Gideon and held out his hand.

"Sheriff, so good to meet you. Won't you please get down from your horse? It is an honor to have you visit my camp. My name is Antonio Cortez," the sheepherder said as he shook Gideon's hand. His English sounded so perfect that only his slight accent gave away the fact that he wasn't speaking his native language.

"I'm Gideon Johann," Gideon said as he climbed off the horse. "Nice to meet you, Mr. Cortez."

"Please call me Antonio. What do I owe the pleasure of your visit?"

"Since you haven't made a visit to town yet, I thought I'd pay you a call. I like to meet new people in the county when I can."

"Can I offer you a drink?"

"Sure."

Cortez made a nod of his head towards the guard. The man hurried into the tent and came out with a bottle of tequila and two glasses. Antonio took the bottle and poured a generous amount of liquor into each glass before handing one to Gideon.

"You don't often see glassware on the trail," Gideon mused before smelling the tequila. He had heard of the liquor, but never before tasted the drink. Tipping up the glass, he took a big swig. The liquor made his mouth pucker and his eyes squinted. "That's a little different than whiskey."

Antonio laughed and slapped his thigh before draining his glass. "Yes, I think you will find that tequila will grow on you. It will teach you Spanish," he said and chuckled some more.

"I wanted to let you know that some other sheepherders that are new to the area had some trouble with area ranchers. They drove sheep off a cliff and killed one of the sheepherders. I think it was probably an accident, but he's still dead nonetheless," Gideon said.

Antonio's grin faded and his face formed a scowl that reminded Gideon of a rattlesnake. "So, are you telling me this because you are on the side of the ranchers and are trying to run me off?"

Gideon rubbed his scar and exhaled. "I'm on the side of the law and I aim to do my best to keep the peace. I only came out here to meet you and to make you aware of the potential for trouble," he said as he stared Antonio in the eye.

"Sheriff, I have men that have been tested in the heat of the battles of war. If these cowboys come riding in here thinking that they are bad men, they may find they've bitten off more than they can chew."

A sinking sensation came over Gideon. He had a feeling that he was stuck in between two opposing forces destined for battle and was impotent to stop any of it. He didn't plan to betray his sentiment and never changed expressions, but held out his glass. "How about I see if that tequila really does help my Spanish," he said before forcing a grin.

Chapter 13

Zack slept late and didn't wake until the smell of bacon cooking aroused him from his lethargy. He quickly threw on his clothes and joined his aunt in the kitchen where she stood at the stove flipping flapjacks and turning eggs. She looked over her shoulder and gave her nephew a quick smile before returning to the cooking.

Sitting down at the table, Zack wondered what could be the occasion. His Aunt Sharon always made sure that he was well fed, but bacon, eggs, flapjacks, and the smell of biscuits in the oven made for a lot to eat. He watched as she heaped food onto two plates and carried them to the table before retrieving the cups of coffee.

"So to what do I owe this pleasure?" Zack asked before taking a bite of bacon.

"I'm making sure my boy is well fed for his departure today," Sharon said.

"You're kicking me out?" Zack asked in surprise.

"No, I'd never kick you out and you know it. I would have been happy if you would have never left here, but that's not the path you chose and rightly so. I'm merely sending you on your way. I've been waiting for you to get up the nerve to do what you came up here for and I think that you might need a little shove," his aunt said and smiled at Zack.

Zack studied his aunt for a moment as he contemplated her words. "Yeah, I suppose you're right. I have enjoyed my time with you though," he said with his mouth full of food and received a reproachful look from his aunt.

"And me with you."

After swallowing a bite of flapjack, he said, "Aunt Sharon, you're not that old. What are you, fifty-two now? You could still find you a companion."

"Zackary Barlow, don't go worrying about me. I have plenty of friends and church to occupy me. I just never needed a man like most women do and I'm way too set in my ways to change now. If I were to marry, you'd probably end up having to break me out of jail after I killed him," she said before taking a sip of coffee.

"This may be my last good meal. Joann is liable to kill me when I show up at the ranch."

"Just be patient. Time is your friend, and time is a healer when someone is ready for it to be."

"Joann used to be so full of life and such a brat. I hardly recognized her by the time she left. What if all that is gone forever?"

"I doubt that to be true. Joann has lost herself, but that part of her is still inside her somewhere. She just has to find it again. Have some faith in her and God. A little praying wouldn't hurt things either. Now eat up. I want you leaving on a full stomach."

After breakfast, Zack packed his belongings and saddled his horse. He walked back into the house and gave his aunt a hug. "Thank you for everything."

His aunt handed him a bag with the remaining biscuits and bacon. "Write me when you get the chance. It's been good having you here again. Love you."

"Love you, too," Zack said before riding away.

Riding east out of town, Zack put his horse into a lope once the animal's muscles warmed and kept the pace up for a couple of miles before slowing. If he pushed hard he probably could make Cheyenne by dark, but he saw no point in trying to do so. He planned to get close enough that he could arrive at the ranch mid-morning the next day.

As he thought about what his aunt had said, he said a silent prayer as he rode. He'd never been much for praying until Mrs. Warf had copied down the scripture for him. Since then he had prayed every time he read the note. The knowledge that two different women had made a point of suggesting prayer had him wondering if the advice could be more than mere coincidence and gave him some comfort.

Thoughts of seeing Joann had his mind racing from one scenario to the next on what he might say and how his wife might respond. He found all the conjecturing exhausting and tried instead to concentrate on improvements he needed to make to the homestead. Thoughts on clearing land didn't seem near as challenging as saving a marriage.

A few miles out of town, he reached the foothills of the Laramie Mountains that he would have to cross to get to Cheyenne. The air turned noticeably colder and pockets of snow still remained in crevices and the shadows. He planned to be well past the range by nightfall and into the rolling prairie where the temperature would be much more suitable for a night spent sleeping on the ground.

The day proved uneventful and even boring. Once he had crossed the mountains, the air warmed to the point that he had to shed his coat. He met a few travelers headed the opposite direction and passed a peddler that tried to flag him down with promises of baubles that would impress any young lady. Towards dusk, Zack found a spring that pooled good water and decided to bed there for the night. After scrounging around to find enough wood to make a fire, he finally got one started and sat by it eating his biscuits and bacon. He figured he remained about ten miles from the Minder ranch and Joann. The thought of being so near made his heart race and his hands feel clammy as he rubbed them together. With nothing to do, he turned in early, tossing in his bedroll for a couple of hours before exhaustion overtook him and he fell to sleep.

With nothing more than stale hardtack to eat for breakfast, Zack didn't linger at his camp. Mounting his horse, he got an early start on the morning. He had never been to the ranch before, but had a pretty good idea of the location from Joann's description of where it lay. The visit from Joann's parents after Tess's death had been the only time that Zack had met the couple. They both had made an effort to get to know him, and he had liked them, but worried over how they would feel about his unannounced arrival.

Zack had been to Cheyenne several times, and when he arrived at a road that he estimated was about four miles from the town, he took it going north, believing it led to his destination. He rode for a half-hour until he came upon an entrance to a ranch. Not sure if he had the right place, he nonetheless began riding onto the property. Just the thought that around the next bend he could run into Joann had him sweating even as the cool morning caused a shiver to travel down his back. After riding over a ridge, he saw a ranch house down below with a barn and corral. A man had a horse tied to a post in the corral and was trying to get the animal to accept a saddle. The wrangler spotted Zack and climbed over the fence to meet his company. At that point, Zack recognized Joann's father.

"Hello, Mr. Minder," Zack said as he rode up.

"Zackary, what a surprise. You've lost too much weight, son. I just about didn't recognize you," Mr. Minder said. "And I told you to call me Jake."

"I guess you know why I'm here," Zack said as he climbed down from his horse.

Jake smiled. "I got a pretty good idea. I can't say that much has changed with Joann. I doubt you'll be well-received."

"I figured as much, but I couldn't stay away any longer. I just had to see her."

"I don't blame you. I wish that girl wasn't so hardheaded. She's got a lot of Abby in her."

"A lot of Abby and Gideon. She got a double dose of hardheadedness," Zack said.

Jake chuckled and shook his head. "When she was little I could put a little fear into her to get her to straighten up, but those days are long gone. That won't work now."

"I know. Where is she?"

"She's with the herd north of here. Come on in the house and have some coffee and breakfast before you ride out there. You look like you haven't had a decent meal in a while. Rita will have a fit when she sees how skinny you are," Jake said as he led Zack to the house.

Rita made a fuss over her son-in-law. Running up, she kissed Zack on the cheek before insisting on fixing him a fresh breakfast. Cold biscuits and warmed over gravy would not do. As Zack ate the freshly prepared meal, the couple sat across from him and talked.

"You're going to shatter Joann's illusion that the past is all behind her," Rita said.

"I had to try something. I couldn't sit waiting in Colorado any longer. Something has to give," Zack said after he finished chewing his bite of food.

"Zack, you're here and there's no turning back now, but I think you came too soon. I still hold out hope that Joann will get a handle on her grief and find her old self, but I don't think it will be today," Rita said in an attempt to soften the blow to his manhood that she felt certain that he would receive.

"Thank you for breakfast. I guess I'm about ready to find out," Zack said as he stood.

Rita had liked Zack from the moment that she first met him. Really, she had liked him from the moment that Joann had first written home about him. The letters had casually mentioned the boy that her daughter had met and something about the writing revealed a different attitude towards the young man than Joann normally held. Even after Joann had returned to Wyoming after her visit to Colorado to finally meet her real father and seemed to have put Zack behind her, Rita knew that she would eventually lose her daughter to Zack all the way down in Colorado. The knowledge had made her happy nonetheless. She knew that her daughter would be loved and cared for by a good man even when Joann could be a brat. As she watched Zack ride off to see Joann, she no longer had the confidence that Zack could make her daughter happy.

Zack spotted the herd and started working his way around it. In a small valley, he found a pond and a saddled horse. At first he didn't see Joann, but as he scouted the spot, he saw her sitting under the branches of a weeping willow. She sat watching the water and didn't see him until his horse nickered a greeting. Joann spun her head towards the sound and jumped up, parting the branches as she shot out from under the tree.

"Hi," Zack said as if it were just another day.

In a surprised voice, Joann asked, "Zack, what are you doing here?"

"I visited Aunt Sharon and wanted to stop in and see you," Zack said even though he detested saying things that were factually true, but misleading as all get out.

"Is your aunt sick?"

"No, I just paid her a visit," Zack said as he climbed off his horse.

"You've lost too much weight," Joann said as she nervously rubbed her palms on her thighs.

"I'm not as good of a cook as you are. Sometimes it seems fixing something to eat is more trouble than it's worth. How have you been?"

"I'm doing fine. I've found a little peace here and I keep busy helping Poppa."

Joann's demeanor surprised him. She remained much calmer than he had expected. He had figured she'd fly into a rage at first sight. She looked good. The sun had tanned some color back onto her face and Rita's cooking had put some curves back on her though he had to look hard to see them under the baggy men's clothing. He ached to hold her and had to force himself to stand back and not embrace his wife.

"I've missed you," Zack said.

"Zack, please don't go there. I'm in a good place here and we've had that conversation way too many times already. I can't go back to the life we had," Joann said and her posture took on the slightest defiant stance.

"But I love you and I dare you to say that you don't love me."

Joann popped her thighs with her hands before pulling her shoulders back as if standing at attention. Her face contorted into a rage. "Love? What does that have to do with anything? If love made the world go round, then me, you, and Tess would all be back home in our cabin being a happy little family. Love can't save anyone. Its only purpose is to cause pain," she shouted.

"You don't really mean that. Every minute we spent loving Tess was worth the pain. Neither of us would ever trade the short time we had with her," Zack said in a soft voice.

"The hell I wouldn't. That's plain crazy talk. If you think spending two and a half weeks loving a baby was worth all this misery then you're out of your mind. Just get out of here. I try not to think about you or Tess and here you show up picking the scab," Joann yelled.

Holding out his arms, Zack took a step towards Joann. "Come here," he said.

"Don't you dare take one more step towards me. You can't fix this with a hug. I meant it when I said I never wanted you to touch me again. I want a divorce. I should have already started it," Joann said in a voice so venomous that Zack stopped in his tracks.

Zack's jaw set and his mouth contorted as he tried to steel himself from the pain. His eyes burned as they began to water. For the first time since Joann had left him, he lost all hope that he'd ever get his wife back. "I'm sorry I bothered you. Send me the papers and I'll sign them. With all my heart, I hope that you find happiness again. I really mean that. You deserve it. Have a good life, Joann. You won't see me again, I can assure of that. This will be my last journey here," he said and turned towards his horse without looking back at his wife again.

Riding back to the ranch, Zack told Joann's parents goodbye. He spared them the details, but told them that he wouldn't be seeing them again. Rita hugged Zack and told him not to lose faith, and Jake shook his hand. As he rode away, he could feel their eyes upon him watching from the porch.

Zack rode south back to the road that led to Cheyenne. He planned to get a room there for the night before beginning his journey back home. A numbness had settled over him and he felt as if he were in a fog as he turned east towards the town. He couldn't even think straight and barely noticed his surroundings.

As he traveled down the road, Zack noticed movement in the brush up ahead. Two riders with pistols drawn emerged from the thicket and blocked his path.

"Well, looky who we have here," one of the men said.

Just as the man spoke, Zack recognized the men as the two outlaws he had whipped when he retrieved the Warf family's possessions. The fog lifted as his mind raced like a lightning bolt through his options. He realized that he was probably going to die, and if he was going to die, he decided that he'd go out fighting. He drew his revolver and just before he pulled the trigger, he heard the roar of the two guns aimed at him. A bullet tore into his pelvis as he fired at the outlaw on his right. The outlaw made a hopping motion in the saddle and Zack shot him again, knocking the robber from the saddle. Spinning his horse to the left to get a better shot, Zack began firing at the second outlaw. The two men were no more than thirty feet apart and shooting at each other as fast as they could cock their revolvers. Zack felt as if someone had waylaid him with a club as a shot grazed his temple and peeled back a chunk of scalp. On his last bullet, he watched the outlaw finally slump over on his horse. The fog descended on him again, and he knew that he had to do something quickly or risk dying in the road. He turned his horse around and galloped back towards the ranch.

The Minder family sat at the table eating lunch. The meal proved a somber affair as Joann had returned from the herd still mad at the world. She quickly told her parents that she had no intentions of discussing the events concerning Zack and expressed her displeasure in them for sending her husband to find her. Joann was the first to hear the sound of the galloping horse. She jumped up from the table in a huff and looked out the window.

"Just what I figured. That fool is coming back for more. You two stay in here and let me handle this. I'll put an end to this nonsense once and for all," Joann said as she marched outside.

Before Zack had gotten close enough even to slow his horse, Joann saw the bright red glistening down the side of his head and down his leg clear to his boot.

"Momma, Poppa, come quick. Zack is hurt," Joann screamed at the top of her lungs.

As the couple ran out onto the porch, Zack yanked his horse to a stop in front of them. He didn't say anything, but looked at them as if he were trying to figure out if he knew them or not.

Jake ran off the porch. "Help me get him down and into the house," he yelled.

Even with Zack's weight loss, it took the effort of all three family members to get him into the house and into Joann's bed.

Joann let out a scream when she looked at Zack's head. "Oh, my God, I can see his skull," she cried out.

Her father looked at Zack's head and moved the flap of skin back to where it belonged. "Don't worry about his head right now. Get his pants off and try to get the bleeding stopped. That's the first thing that needs to be done. I'm going to go get the doctor," he said before leaving the room. He grabbed his gun belt and headed towards the barn to saddle his best horse.

Rita retrieved a pair of scissors, and after they pulled off Zack's boots, she began cutting his pants and long underwear from the bottom up until she could pull the material back. The gaping wound still oozed blood.

"Get some clean towels," Rita barked out at Joann as her daughter stood frozen in the corner.

Joann ran out of the room and returned with an arm full of towels. She handed one to her mother. "What if he dies? I was so mean to him today. I'll never forgive myself if he does."

"You need to worry about keeping him alive right now and not think about the other. You never know when the last time you might see someone is," her mother said as she cut a towel into a piece small enough to plug into the wound. Zack let out a groan as she inserted the material, but no longer opened his eyes.

"Momma, he's such a good man. Why would somebody do this?"

"I don't know. Grab a towel and apply pressure to the wound. Not too much though. I'm going to get some water and clean his head," Rita said before leaving.

Jake put his horse into a lope towards Cheyenne. As he came upon the scene of the shootout, he saw a man on the right side of the road lying dead. On the left side, a second man sat propped up against a rock.

"Hey, mister, can you help me? My partner and I got ambushed. I think a bullet busted my shoulder," the man called out.

Climbing down from his horse, Jake surveyed the scene. He relaxed a little when he saw that the man's gun rested out of reach. The man must have noticed all the blood smeared on Jake as his eyes suddenly grew large.

"That is my son-in-law you shot, and he would never ambush anybody if his life depended on it, you good for nothing son of a bitch," Jake yelled.

The outlaw flopped over and tried to reach his gun on the ground, but didn't have the strength to get to it. Jake had never pointed a gun at another human being in his life. He calmly pulled out his revolver and cocked the gun. Aiming at the man's heart, he fired his pistol. The outlaw groaned and flung backwards, dead with a bullet to the chest.

Mounting his horse and looking down on the body, Jake said, "You'll never ruin another life, you bastard."

Chapter 14

Doctor Walters arrived at the Minder ranch by horseback. He preferred riding to using a carriage like most doctors favored. The doctor had been a young decorated surgeon during the war and had treated more gunshot wounds in a week of battles than most doctors saw in a lifetime. He had a neatly trimmed mustache with long sideburns and always dressed in a black long coat with a string tie. His black boots somehow remained shiny and dust free no matter the weather conditions. Though well regarded for his medical skills, most people did not take to the physician. He maintained a detached superiority towards his patients, and if someone addressed him as Doc, he would correct them that he preferred to be called Doctor Walters.

Rita led the doctor to the bedroom where Joann continued to hold pressure on the wound. Zack had lost all shades of color and looked ghostly pale. He opened his eyes occasionally and mumbled nonsense, but Rita and Joann doubted that he recognized either of them.

"Please stand back while I perform an examination," the doctor requested.

He removed the towel and grabbed a pair of forceps from his bag to retrieve the material that Rita had shoved into the wound. With the removal of the cloth came a mess of coagulating goo.

"Can we get more light into this room? I need to wash my hands," Walters said as he headed to the pump in the kitchen to scrub.

By the time the doctor returned to the bedroom, four oil lamps had been placed about the room, brightening it considerably. Doctor Walters disinfected his hands and then inserted his finger into the wound and probed. Zack furrowed his brow, but made no real sign of discomfort.

Jake walked into the room. He had just returned home after stopping by the jail to inform the sheriff of the shooting after he had summoned the doctor.

"Good," the doc said at seeing Jake. "I'd prefer not to give this young man any anesthesia or to drug him. He's lost a tremendous amount of blood. Mr. Minder, I want you to sit on his chest and hold him down. The ladies may each have to grab a leg."

Retrieving a scalpel, the doctor made two quick slices into the gunshot to widen the opening. Zack barely stirred. Doctor Walters inserted the forceps into the wound and probed for only a moment before extracting the bullet. He inserted his finger again and retrieved what looked like a glob of blood until he flattened the object on a towel to reveal a piece of Zack's pants.

Joann and Rita each held one of Zack's legs though he had made no attempt to struggle. Watching the doctor work, Joann could feel her stomach in her throat. Doctor Walters had been her doctor since childhood and she knew he'd show no compassion if she puked all over the place. She focused her attention on Zack's face. Her eyes welled with tears as she looked at her injured husband. Her mind jumped to the first time that Zack had kissed her. He'd been so shy that he first asked permission, and as she always did to him, she made things difficult, but the kiss had made sparks fly. Now so many emotions were running through her that she felt almost as overwhelmed as she did by watching the surgery. She felt guilt, love, loss, and resignation that life could never be easy before saying a silent prayer for Zack's recovery.

Doctor Walters inserted his finger back into the wound. He twisted it around in the hole until satisfied that all material had been retrieved. The doctor paused to feel Zack's neck to check his pulse.

"I'm going to have to tie off an artery in his pelvis. I believe he will bleed to death otherwise," the doctor said as he began threading a needle with catgut suture.

The doctor made a loop of the suture and used his forceps to guide the catgut into the wound and over the severed artery. With a nimble touch, he quickly tied off the blood vessel. Moving on to the incisions he had made, Doctor Walter stitched the cuts back together, but left the gunshot wound open. Zack stirred as the doctor worked, but didn't offer to resist. The doctor finished by drenching the wound in carbolic acid and bandaging it before pausing.

"Baring infection, the wound will heal fine. The loss of blood is a concern. I'll see about his head now. What is this man's name again?" Doctor Walters asked in his clinical manner.

"Zack Barlow. He's my husband," Joann said a little louder than she intended.

"Yes, Zack. It is a good thing he is a stout young man or he would already be dead," the doctor said as he pulled back the flap of skin torn loose from Zack's head. "The bullet marked his skull. That's as close to getting your brains blown out as you can come."

Retrieving scissors from his bag, the doctor clipped Zack's hair to the skin around the wound and on the flap. After threading his needle with fresh suture, he began to stitch the flap of skin back in place.

"So, do any of you know what happened? The other two men will keep the secret for eternity," the doctor said as he methodically worked.

Joann and Rita looked up at Jake in surprise.

"I believe he was ambushed by a couple of highwaymen. The sheriff said they were looking for a couple of men that fit the description that I gave him of them. Zack apparently ended their careers of crime. He did some work as a deputy in Colorado," Jake answered.

"Good for him. I have no tolerance for those types of men," Doctor Walters said as he knotted off the suture.

The doctor grabbed an oil lamp and held it in front of Zack's face as he pried an eye open. He repeated the procedure with the other eye before returning the lamp back to the dresser. After pulling out his stethoscope, he listened to Zack's heart and chest before returning the instrument to his bag.

"Zack is in severe shock from loss of blood and trauma. He also has a bad concussion. I hope that there will be no brain swelling. I wouldn't expect it, but cannot rule out the possibility. He probably will not be coherent for a couple of days if he is awake at all. Zack is a strong young man and capable of making a full recovery, but we will have to see how his body responds in the next couple of days to all the stress it has been put under. Get as much water down him as possible and food if he will eat it," Doctor Walters said. "I will return to check on him tomorrow."

The family walked the doctor out of the house and watched him ride away.

"So tell us what you found," Rita said to her husband.

"On the way into town I found two men that I assume Zack killed when they tried to rob him. The sheriff is going to retrieve the bodies, but he sounded pretty sure that they were the men that he has been trying to catch," Jake answered.

"Why didn't the fool just let them rob him?" Joann asked.

"Joann," Rita admonished.

"I'd say that he thought he would die if he didn't fight. Sounds like a pretty brave man to me," Jake said before leading his horse away to the barn.

"I'm going to go sit with Zack in case he wakes up and is confused," Joann said as she and her mother returned into the home.

"I guess you're going to have him in your hair a little longer than you planned," Rita said.

"I certainly hope so. I never wished him dead," Joann said before darting back to the bedroom.

She grabbed the scissors off the dresser and finished cutting away Zack's pants. She removed some coins, a penknife, and a bloodstained note from his pockets. The note piqued her curiosity. She unfolded the paper and read aloud, "Do not be anxious about anything, but in everything by prayer and supplication with thanksgiving let your requests be made known to God."

Joann grabbed a chair and pulled it over to the bed. As she sat down, she read the bible verse again. The creases were well worn as if Zack read the note often. She wondered if he had been praying for her and their marriage. The handwriting looked unfamiliar. It certainly wasn't Zack or Abby's hand. She didn't know what to make of the verse as she set it down with his other belongings.

Leaning over, Joann kissed Zack on the forehead and took his hand. "Zack, I'm sorry I was so mean to you today. I know you've always had a hard time trying to figure me out and certainly more so after we lost Tess. Maybe I don't understand myself, but I know how I felt. I just couldn't go on as before. No matter what, I'll never stop loving you and I can't imagine never seeing you again. Get well for me. All right?"

Chapter 15

Sitting in front of the jail, Gideon took the last drag on his cigar before crushing it under his boot heel. The night before he had dreamed about Tess. The after effect had hung over him like a cloud all day. What he needed was somebody to talk with until his mood cleared away. He tried to chat with Abby at breakfast, but Chance had a stomachache and his wife's preoccupation with the child had made conversation impossible. Finnie had been itching to take a ride so Gideon had sent him to check on the Laxalt brothers to see if they had had any more trouble with ranchers. And Doc had a steady stream of patients coming in and out of his office.

Gideon pulled his hat down snugly and walked down the alley to the back door of the Last Chance. Mary sat at the wooden table pouring over the business ledgers. She looked up and smiled at seeing the sheriff as he ambled over and plopped into a chair.

"How bad is the Pearl West hurting your business?" Gideon asked as he pushed his hat back and reclined the chair on two legs.

"Well, it hasn't done us any favors, but it's not as bad as I feared it would be. We're still making money. It seems most everybody prefers to drink here. We have better liquor and beer. We take a beating on the ranch hand's payday though. They head to the Pearl West to blow their wages on girls and gambling. The restaurant does better all the time. The stigma of a retired whore running it has about worn off. More of the town's ladies eat there all the time," Mary said.

"Good. I wasn't sure how you'd fare against that place. How's Sam?"

"Growing. He eats, sleeps, and poops. That's about the extent of it," she said with a laugh.

"They get a lot more fun when they start moving around a little bit."

"All right, Mr. Johann, what's troubling you? Don't waste my time denying it. I can see pain all over your face," Mary said before closing her ledger.

Gideon let out a little snicker and leaned back farther in his chair. Mary's ability to read his moods had always been a source of wonder and annoyance to him. He leaned forward to put the chair back on all fours. "I dreamed about Tess last night and I can't shake the feeling. How can a dream hold such power? I feel as if the funeral happened just yesterday."

"I don't know, but they just do. The other night I dreamed about the time that cowboy beat the hell out of me. I hadn't thought about that in forever. It put me in a dark mood all day and I about bit Finnie's head off. Tess hasn't been gone very long and it's still raw. It also doesn't help that Joann has struggled so. Things will get better, but you'll never get over that loss. You will learn to live with it and I hope Joann will do the same."

Forcing a smile, Gideon said, "Pretty sage advice for a saloonkeeper."

"That wasn't the saloonkeeper talking. That was the orphan and the whore. Being either one of them will teach you just about anything you need to know about human nature."

"Life isn't for sissies, that's for sure," Gideon mused.

"No, it isn't. On a better note, I think I've got String Callow talked into going to see Abby about a job."

"I've been meaning to ask you about that."

"Yeah, String took a little more convincing than I thought he would. I've been working on him."

"Abby needs to get something done. We have too many head of cattle for somebody not to be watching over them."

"There's one more thing that you need to know," Mary said as she walked to a cabinet and retrieved a bottle of whiskey and a glass. She poured three fingers worth and sat the drink in front of Gideon. "The ranchers are getting all their cowboys riled up about the sheepherders. They have them believing that they'll be out of business and the cowboys out of work. That's all every ranch hand that comes in the Last Chance wants to talk about."

Gideon took a swallow of the whiskey and allowed a moment to pass while he savored the taste. "I knew things had been too quiet. There wasn't any way this was going to go away."

"No, I don't think so. What do you intend to do?"

"I haven't a clue. Finnie and I can't stop a war without help and we won't get any help until there's a war," he said, smiling sadly at his play on words.

"I'm sorry. I should have told you on a better day. My job is to make you feel better."

Tipping back the glass, Gideon drained the whiskey. "I prefer hearing it on a bad day rather than ruin a good one."

Mary let out a chuckle. "That certainly is an interesting way to look at it. Even on a bad day, you're an optimist. The old Gideon would never have thought that way."

"I don't want to think anymore today, especially about the old me. Let me know if you hear that something is imminent," Gideon said as he stood.

∞

Winnie herded Chance back into the cabin. Abby had sent the children outside only a few minutes before to play while insisting that they needed to enjoy the last of the fall weather.

"Winnie, what are you doing back in here?" Abby asked her daughter.

"There's a rider coming and it's not Gideon," Winnie said.

Abby reached for the shotgun above the door. After a crazed preacher had tried to harm her and the children as revenge directed at Gideon, she found herself overly cautious when visitors arrived unexpectedly. Each time that she grabbed the gun, she tried to convince herself that she wouldn't do the same thing the next time so that she wouldn't frighten the children, but she never did.

"It's probably nothing. Just keep Chance inside while I see what they want," Abby said as she walked out onto the porch with the shotgun resting in the crook of her arm.

"Ma'am, my name is String Callow. I heard that you were looking for a good ranch hand and I wanted to make my availability known to you," the rider said from atop his horse while holding his hat in his hand.

The first thing that crossed Abby's mind was that String certainly appeared to be an appropriate name. The cowboy appeared as if he might be even taller than Ethan and looked as rawboned as a chicken leg after Gideon had finished gnawing it. She guessed him to be about thirty years old. A good age to her way of thinking – young enough to still be able to work hard, yet old enough to have gained some smarts. His appearance and clothing were certainly better and cleaner than most of the ranch hands she had seen. Still, she found him showing up for a job unannounced to be an odd circumstance.

"How did you hear about the job?" Abby asked.

"Last Stand isn't much of a town for secrets, ma'am," String answered.

Abby smiled for the first time. "You certainly are right about that. Do you have a job now?"

"I work on the Harris Ranch. I'd be a better foreman than what they got, but I'll never get the chance. I kind of like the idea of being out here and on my own."

"You wouldn't be on your own. You would be taking orders from me," Abby said.

"Oh, I know that you're the boss, but I don't need daily instructions. I figured we could work together on the big decisions and you could let me take care of the day-to-day things," String said in his easy manner.

"That's a bit presumptuous of you, don't you think?"

"Ma'am, are you aiming to shoot me or is it safe that I climb down from my horse?" String asked.

"Only if you give me reason to shoot you. I know how to use this thing. You may step down though. Do you know Gideon?"

"I don't know the sheriff well. I've talked to him a couple of times in the saloon," he answered as he climbed off his horse.

"I don't know you from Adam. How do I know I can trust you?" she boldly asked.

"Mary Ford likes me. People claim that she's a pretty fair judge of character."

Hearing Mary's name mentioned was like a revelation. "Mary is the one that talked you into coming out here, didn't she?"

String's face turned red and he stammered. "She might have suggested it," he finally said.

Sitting her shotgun against the rail of the porch, Abby sat down in the swing. She thought the world of Mary and knew that her friend was only looking out for her and Gideon's best interest, but nonetheless, she would have liked to have found a ranch hand all on her own. On the other hand, there wasn't anything better than Mary Ford's seal of approval.

"String, why don't you come sit down up here and let's see if we can make this work or not," Abby said.

Chapter 16

Zack had spent the better part of two days sleeping. He would wake up long enough that Joann and Rita would force some soup and water down him, but his conversations were largely incoherent. Occasionally he would call out for his Aunt Sharon. Doctor Walters had made a point of coming out to the ranch each day to check on his patient and seemed satisfied with the young man's progress. The doctor kept reassuring the family that he believed that Zack would regain his mental faculties.

Joann hadn't left the house since her husband had arrived. She had continuously peppered her father, mother, and the doctor with questions concerning what they thought about Zack's chances for a recovery. Her mother, tired of watching her daughter pace the floor, had tried to get her to go help her father, but Joann felt obligated to stay to care for Zack. She also secretly feared that he could take a turn for the worse and she wanted to be by his side in such an event.

Walking into the bedroom with a bowl of soup, Joann clinked the spoon against the dishware. Zack opened his eyes and gazed at his wife.

"I suppose you think I got shot to stay around you a little longer," he said and made a weak attempt at a smile.

"Do you know me?" Joann asked as she leaned over Zack.

"Well, of course, I know you. I didn't get shot in the head."

"Actually, you did get shot in the head. You've been babbling for two days."

Zack reached up to touch his wound and winced. "Am I going to be a simpleton?"

All the worrying that Joann had endured since the shooting gave way and she started to giggle. The relief felt so immense that she had a hard time stopping and had to gasp for breath between fits of laughter. She even snorted through her nose like a pig. Finally, she said, "I've thought you a simpleton for quite some time now."

Looking at his wife in confusion, Zack said, "Seriously, am I going to be all right?"

"The doctor thinks you will make a full recovery, but it will take some time. You lost a lot of blood. Your head should heal fine and maybe your new hairstyle will become fashionable. What happened?"

Thinking for a moment as he recalled the gunfight, Zack recounted all that had led up to his crossing paths with the outlaws for a second time. At the end of the account, he asked, "What happened to the outlaws?"

"You killed them both. The sheriff had been looking for them," Joann answered.

"I knew I hit them, but I didn't stick around to see how badly they were wounded. I thought I was going to bleed out before I got here."

"You lost consciousness when you got here. We were scared to death that you were going to die before the doctor could arrive. Momma and I tried to stop the bleeding and Poppa got the doctor."

"I'm much obliged for all your family has done for me."

"Where did the bible verse in your pocket come from?"

Failing at his attempt to hide his embarrassment at the discovery of the note, he said, "Mrs. Warf wrote that out for me for helping them out. They were such a nice family."

"So what have you been praying for?" Joann asked coyly.

"I think prayers are probably like wishes on a falling star and better kept to myself."

"Well, no matter what, I'm just happy that you are doing better. I really worried that your mind might be touched," she said. "Now let me feed you some soup."

"I can feed myself," he said as he attempted to prop himself up in the bed.

Joann grabbed an extra pillow and helped get him to a reclining position. "I've been inside this house since you were shot to take care of you and I will not be denied. I'm going to feed you whether you like it or not. Besides, you know I always get my way," she said with a grin as she directed a spoonful of soup towards Zack's mouth.

"Are you still mad at me for showing up here?"

"Well, I can't see where you getting yourself nearly killed accomplished very much. You should have been back home in Colorado taking care of the homestead," she said before quickly shoveling another spoonful of soup into her husband in hopes that he wouldn't notice that she still called Colorado home.

"Joann, I'm sorry for whatever mistakes I made in our marriage. I really tried, but I know I fell short."

"Zackary Barlow, you were as fine of a husband as any girl could want. If anyone should apologize, I think we both know it should be me. I am the brat. I like being a brat, and truth be told, you probably liked me being one, too, but that isn't what this is about at all. I found out that I'm not near as strong of a person as I thought I was. Tess's death shattered that illusion and I've decided that I'm not capable of dealing with that kind of grief ever again. You getting shot has only made me more convinced that I'm right. I've worried myself to death about you. I might not be able to still be your wife, but I certainly want you alive and happy."

Rita stood outside the doorway eavesdropping on the conversation. Disappointed in what her daughter had to say, she had hoped Zack's near death would bring Joann to her senses. Her only consolation was in the fact that Joann's voice did not have near the conviction to it that it had in the past when she and her daughter had argued over Joann's decision to leave Zack to come back to the Wyoming Territory.

Chapter 17

With the help of Delta, Mary had the Last Chance ready to open for the usual busy Saturday crowd. The saloon owner did a quick glance around the room and decided she had the time to walk down to the jail to talk to Gideon before she opened. She would have given the message to Finnie, but he had been fast asleep when she had returned home the previous night and she had been likewise when he left for the jail that morning. As she threw on her shawl to walk out the door, Cyrus Capello walked into the saloon.

"Good morning, ma'am. I'm Cyrus Capello. I'm the owner of the Pearl West and I'm looking to speak with Mrs. Ford," he said with exaggerated formality.

Mary had seen Cyrus walking down the street before, but this was her first up close encounter. She couldn't take her eyes off his hair and wondered what would happen if he got too close to a candle and all that pomade ignited. "That would be me. Have a seat. Can I offer you something to drink?" she asked as Delta made herself scarce by darting off to the back room.

"No thank you, I'm good," Cyrus said as he moved to a chair at the nearest table and waited for Mary to take a seat.

"What can I do for you, Mr. Capello?" Mary asked as she scooted her seat up to the table.

"Mrs. Ford, I'm one for cutting to the chase. I'm finding that your saloon is a hard habit to break for these old cowboys. I would like to buy the Last Chance.

I'm willing to make you a very generous offer," Cyrus said in a measured tone.

Mary looked Cyrus in the eyes trying to get a read on the man. His offer had come so far out of the blue that she found herself completely caught off guard. She could feel her heart racing in her chest and she kept her hands resting on the table for fear they might betray her with a tremble. Clearing her throat, she said, "Mr. Capello, don't you think it is a little early to be trying to eliminate your competition? You haven't been open very long."

"That is all true, but I like to think of myself as a man of action. I don't like the results so far and would rather take steps to remedy the situation."

"I love this saloon. A kind man left me this place and changed my life. I couldn't ever sell the Last Chance."

"Don't you want to hear my offer?" Cyrus asked, his voice rising slightly in pitch and volume.

"No, I do not," she said firmly.

Cyrus eyes flashed and his grin looked sinister. He leaned closer. His appearance reminded Mary of a rattlesnake ready to strike.

"Mrs. Ford, I respect your spirit, but Cyrus Capello usually gets what he is after. We are not finished yet. We will be talking again," he said as he arose from the table.

Mary stood and walked towards the bar. "Mr. Capello, I want to show you something," she said as she pointed down at the bar. "I blew a chunk out of my bar when I blew out the brains of the last man that thought he could force me to sell."

Cyrus turned on his heels and marched out the door.

Pulling her shawl tight, Mary took a deep breath and exhaled calmly before walking outside. She walked slowly and with purpose to the jail and entered. Gideon and Finnie were both sitting back in their chairs with their feet up on the desk. Finnie puffed away on a cigar and Gideon blew plumes of smoke from his pipe. Smoke hung in the room like a brush fire gone out of control. Mary swatted at the cloud in a futile attempt to find some breathable air.

"My God, how do you two heathens breathe?" Mary asked.

"Top of the morning to you, my love. We inhale around the smoke," Finnie said with a chuckle.

Propping the door open before taking a seat, Mary said, "This is worse than the saloon ever gets."

After blowing out a puff of smoke, Gideon said, "Our goal is to keep the cold out and not try to heat the outside."

"Well, your new goal is to make sure I stay happy with some fresh air and I know that both of you are smart enough not to fail at that," Mary said and nodded her head with finality.

"As the sheriff and deputy of this fine county, how may we serve you?" Gideon asked.

"There's going to be trouble sometime today. I don't know when or which sheepherder that they're planning on hitting. I just heard enough table talk to know that something is happening. Some of the ranch hands were beside themselves with excitement. I couldn't exactly ask questions."

Gideon and Finnie's boots hit the floor in unison as they sat up straight in their chairs.

"Oh, that's not good," Finnie said as he shook his head.

"I wish we had an idea of how many men we are dealing with," Gideon said.

"I wish I had more information, but the conversations were pretty hushed. Only the beer kicking in gave them away."

"We at least know that something is up," Gideon said.

"Changing the subject, I just had the oddest encounter. Cyrus Capello just came into the Last Chance and tried to buy it from me. When I said no, I swear his head looked as if it turned into that of a rattler. That's an evil man, I tell you," Mary said.

Finnie stood. "Did he threaten you?" he asked, his voice rising with emotion.

"Not really. He told me he usually gets what he wants so I proceeded to show him where I killed Hiatt."

"Good for you. That's showing him," Gideon said.

Taking a step past Mary, Finnie said, "I'm going over there right now and put an end to this. That dago better watch himself."

Rubbing his scar, Gideon said, "Finnie, wait. Let Cyrus lick his wounds before you go running over there. You'll just make him more determined. He might be evil, but he's not stupid. He knows that harming any of you would be a death sentence. Let's wait and see if this is the end of it."

Mary grabbed Finnie's hand. "Gideon is right. It's never wise to poke a snake. Let him be."

Finnie walked back to his seat and dropped into it. "You two better be right. I'll kill the son of a bitch if he messes with us."

Standing, Mary said, "I have to get back to the saloon. Worry about what's going to happen tonight and not about Cyrus Capello." She leaned over and kissed Finnie before walking out the door.

Bending forward, Finnie said, "Lewis Wise seems to be the ringleader on all this. Are we going to ride out to see him to try to stop this nonsense?"

"I don't think it would do any good. They'd just pick another day and we might not get a heads-up on it the next time. I don't want a massacre on our hands," Gideon said.

"Things would be considerably easier if we didn't have a conscience about this whole thing. We could conveniently look away."

"That it would. Those sheepherders aren't doing anything to keep us in a job. But us being the honorable sort that we are and seeing how that we took an oath to uphold the law, I guess that isn't in the cards," Gideon said with a grin.

"Which bunch do you think they'll go after?"

"Since the Mexican is well-armed, I'm guessing they'll hit the Laxalt brothers again. We'll warn the Mexican and try to protect the brothers. We had better get out there. Since last night was the start of a new moon, I can't imagine that they'll be doing this at night in that kind of darkness."

"We're liable to be facing more men than in a whorehouse on Saturday night," Finnie said as he stood.

"We'll give them a bigger bang for their buck," Gideon said as he picked up his hat from his desk and dropped it onto his head.

The two lawmen rode out of town and easily followed the trail of barren ground until they came upon the same guard that Gideon had encountered on his first visit. Offering no resistance, the sentinel led them to the relocated tent of Antonio Cortez.

Cortez emerged from the tent as impeccably dressed as before and offered a hearty greeting to both Gideon and Finnie.

"Sheriff, did you come for more tequila or are you here on business?" Antonio asked, laughing afterward.

"I think there is going to be trouble today. I don't know whether it will be directed at you or at the Laxalt brothers southwest of here. Have you met the brothers?" Gideon asked.

The big grin faded from Antonio's face. "No, I haven't met them. One of my guards occasionally checks on their whereabouts. Either way this is bad for both of the flocks."

"Exactly. Finnie and I are going to go protect the brothers. Their shotguns will be useless if the ranchers decide to pick them off from a distance. At least you and your men will know to keep a sharp eye out."

"Sheriff, take Sid and Roberto with you. They will even things out a little."

Gideon glanced towards the two men standing near Antonio. Both men had the battle scars to prove their merit in a fight and the sheriff knew that he wouldn't want to meet either man in a dark alley. Neither betrayed the least bit of emotion concerning their bosses offering their services.

"They would have to follow my orders. I'm going to try to keep from getting anybody killed," Gideon said.

"They will take orders from you," Antonio said before looking at his two men and nodding his head with authority.

"All right, then, let's go," Gideon said. "And thank you, Antonio."

The four men rode away towards the area where the Laxalt brothers grazed their sheep. They first found Ander tending his flock, and after some awkward sign language, the sheepherder pointed them in the direction of Dominique.

As Gideon rode up on the sheepherder, Dominique pulled his shotgun off his shoulder and held the gun across his chest as he nervously eyed the two strangers accompanying the lawmen.

"You can put your gun away. Nobody is here to hurt you," Gideon said as he climbed down off Buck.

"What bring you out here?" Dominque asked.

"I think there's going to be trouble today. These men have come to help. I want you and Peru to move your flocks in with Ander's sheep and then come with me."

"I told you before I not run no more. I fight this time."

"Dominque, the ranchers could kill you with a rifle, and your shotgun wouldn't even reach them. Ander is in a nice valley with good cover on the north side. We can hide there and protect you and your sheep. Getting yourself killed won't accomplish a damn thing," Gideon said in a reassuring voice.

"I no coward," Dominque said, his voice rising.

"No, you are not, but we have to do this my way. Either do what I ask or I'm going to arrest you and your brothers," Gideon said as he stared the sheepherder in the eye.

"Arrest for what?" Dominque asked excitedly.

"It doesn't matter, but I'm not going to let any of you die if I can help it."

"I no like this, but you give me no choice," Dominque said before yelling commands to his dogs.

After combining the three flocks, Gideon stationed the men on a ridge on the north side of the valley that provided a clear view of the whole valley and the exposed entry from the south. His plan called for him and Finnie to shoot the horses out from under the first two men that charged the flock with hopes that the rest of the riders would scatter.

Sid and Roberto walked up to Gideon carrying their Sharps fifty caliber rifles.

"You should use these first," Sid said as he offered Gideon the gun. "We can gain at least a hundred yards if not more ground before they reach the flock. It should give the ranchers plenty of time to think about how much they really want to cause trouble."

"Are you and Roberto good with those Sharps?" Gideon asked.

Sid smiled. "We can gain you two hundred yards," he said.

"Very well. You two take the first two shots, but not until I say so and don't shoot again unless I give the go ahead."

Nodding his head, Sid turned and walked off to his position. Roberto did the same.

For the next two hours, the men sat and watched the sheep graze. Gideon would occasionally scan the horizon with his spyglass. The three sheepherders nervously moved about while the seasoned fighters remained calm and in position. The sun would soon be dipping behind the rim of the valley.

"Maybe they are waiting until dark," Finnie called out.

"I doubt it. There's still plenty of time. They are probably planning on it being dark by the time word gets back to town."

Twenty minutes later, ten riders with gunnysacks over their heads came charging towards the flock from the south. The large number of men surprised Gideon as he watched them advance. He gave the order for the guards to shoot when they were ready and hoped that he wouldn't have a bloodbath on his hands.

The two Sharps rifles fired with their unmistakable roar. Gideon watched and waited for the delay between the sound of the guns and the bullets reaching their target to see if the guards had hit their mark. A horse reared up on its hind legs, throwing the rider, before toppling. A second horse gave a little jump into the air before continuing to run until its knees buckled and it ran itself into the ground. Two of the other riders pulled their mounts up hard to a stop, but the other men continued their charge towards the flock. The ranchers were still well over a hundred yards from the sheep and out of range of Gideon and Finnie's Winchesters.

"Take down two more horses," Gideon yelled.

Wasting no time, the Sharps roared again. A horse buckled at the knees, sending its rider catapulting through the air. The airborne cowboy flapped his arms as if he were trying to fly before crashing to the ground. The second shot appeared to have missed the mark. All of the riders now came to a quick stop before turning their attention to the horseless men. The cowboy that had been launched through the air staggered around as if lost and had to be helped onto the back of a saddle. With the men retrieved, the riders made a hasty retreat.

"Nobody killed. I'd say that those boys will head home with their tails tucked between their legs," Finnie hollered out.

"I think so, too" Gideon said.

Sid and Roberto got into a brief argument over which one had missed with their shot before realizing that they both had aimed at the same horse. Wishing to keep the peace, nobody bothered to check the dead animal for multiple gunshots.

After waiting another half-hour to make sure the riders did not return, Gideon let the Laxalt brothers return to their sheep. He and Finnie rode back with the two guards to see Antonio Cortez.

"I believe I heard the Sharps rifles," Antonio said.

"Yes, you did. Those guns came in pretty handy and we didn't have to kill anyone. I think I have the ranchers where I want them now. They'll have to listen to me."

"What do you propose?"

"Most of the ranches are south of here. I'm going to look at a map and come up with a boundary between sheep and cattle. You won't get the best of the land, but there's still plenty of territory to graze your flocks. It sure beats a war. Would you agree to that?"

Antonio spoke to Roberto in Spanish and the only word Gideon understood was tequila. Roberto dashed into the tent and returned with five glasses and a fresh bottle of the liquor.

Taking the bottle, Antonio said, "Gentlemen, let's drink to today's success and a possible deal to prevent bloodshed." The Mexican began filling the glasses with the liquor.

Finnie nudged Gideon. "I swore off whiskey for Mary. Do you think tequila would be cheating?" he asked.

"No, it's not like you can find the stuff anywhere but here with Senor Cortez. I don't think he will let you stay with him once he gets to know you."

Antonio let out a laugh. "Senor Finnie, you must have one very special lady or else one very mean one," he said as all the men chuckled.

"Actually, she is both. She is a wonderful woman and as mean as a snake," Finnie said, causing more laughter.

All of the men took their glass and Antonio toasted, "Prosperity to all." With a click of the glasses, the men drained their drinks.

Before Antonio could fill the glasses again, Gideon said, "We would love to stay and drink with you, but we have to get back to town. I expect there's a busted up cowboy in the doctor's office right now and I want to catch him on the spot."

"Very well, Senor Gideon. I make no promises on our little treaty, but I am willing to listen," Antonio said.

"That's all I can ask for," Gideon said before he and Finnie rode away.

As the lawmen loped towards town, Finnie hollered, "Sid and Roberto are pretty fair shots with those Sharps."

"Yes, they are. We're not going to tell anybody about that. Things will be better if the ranchers think that we did the shooting. The less they know the better. I think we'll find Lewis Wise in Doc's office. That last horse they shot was Lewis's appaloosa."

"I kind of liked that tequila, but I bet that stuff would make for one bad hangover."

Gideon chuckled. "I would say so and I sure wouldn't want to find out, but it's probably no worse than what will happen when Mary finds out that she is meaner than a snake."

"Like the one whore said to the other – it's best not to tell what you do in your room or how much you charge for the pleasure," Finnie said.

"I don't even know what your point is."

"You're not the smartest man I ever met, but you're no fool. I have a thing or two I could tell Abby, too."

"And how did that metaphor apply to that?"

"It means it's best to keep your mouth shut. I thought that it sounded pretty good," Finnie answered.

"God bless Mary for putting up with you," Gideon said and shook his head.

In town, two horses stood tied in front of the doctor's office. Gideon and Finnie walked in and found Carter Mason sitting on the bench and Lewis Wise up on the table with his head bandaged and Doc tying the bindings on a splint over the rancher's arm.

Walking up to Carter, Gideon said, "Carter, I expected better of you. You're a reasonable man and know full well that those sheepherders have as much right to the open range as you do."

Carter looked down at his feet and began twirling the end of his handlebar mustache. "I know," he said quietly.

"How badly is he hurt, Doc?" Gideon asked.

"A knot on his head with some stitches and a broken arm. He's going to be mighty sore for a few days," Doc answered.

"You had no right to shoot my horse out from under me. I could have broken my neck. And that was a fine horse you killed. That was the best cattle horse I owned. How'd you know we were coming?" Lewis asked.

"If you would have had that horse out herding cattle instead of trying to scatter sheep, it would still be alive. And I had every right to protect those sheepherders from a slaughter. I've been watching them. I knew it was only a matter of time before you did something stupid again."

"You're awfully full of yourself," Lewis said.

"Lewis, you seem to be the ringleader of all this trouble. Monday morning I'm going to go talk to District Attorney Kile and we're going to come up with every charge we can think of against you – maybe even the murder of Julen Laxalt. And then I'm coming out to your place and you can decide on whether you want to agree to some boundaries between cattle and sheep or if you'd prefer to take up residence at the jail. You will also get all the other ranchers on board with this settlement. Do you understand?" Gideon said as he moved close to Lewis.

Staring at Gideon, Lewis said, "There's always another sheriff's election."

Gideon used his finger and thumb to flick Lewis on his head wound. "You better decide if you want peace or a jail cell."

"Damn, Gideon. That hurt. I'll see you Monday," Lewis said.

Chapter 18

As church let out Sunday morning, Sarah pulled Abby aside. "Why don't you let me take Winnie and Chance home with us for the afternoon? This is liable to be the last time the weather will be warm enough for Benjamin and Winnie to play outside until spring. You took Benjamin last time and you and Gideon could use some alone time."

"Really? You want Chance too?" Abby asked skeptically.

"Sure. I haven't had my fill of a little one in a long time. I could use it."

"Sarah, he's a good boy, but such a hand full. He's so busy," Abby warned.

"Abby, I been around a child or two in my time. I want to have him."

Gideon and Ethan walked up to where their wives stood.

"Sarah wants to take the children for the afternoon," Abby said to Gideon.

Looking skeptical, Gideon said, "You don't know what Chance is like."

Ethan waved his hand in the air. "Nonsense. Sarah and I talked about it this morning while getting ready for church. Now that Benjamin is older, we never get to spend time with a little one. Sarah and I both miss that. And we do remember what little boys are like."

Nodding her head towards Benjamin, Sarah said, "Let us enjoy Chance. By the time Benjamin is old enough to have children, we may be too old to enjoy them."

Benjamin and Winnie stood near the wagon talking in conspiratorial tones. "And besides, I fear I'm going to have to share those grandkids with you anyway."

"You won't have to twist my arm. Thank you," Abby said.

Riding home on the buckboard, Gideon grinned and asked, "So what are we going to do to amuse ourselves this afternoon?"

Abby slapped him on the shoulder. "Get that silly grin off your face. The first thing we're going to do is take a horse ride and check on String. Your behavior will determine what amusing things we may get into later."

Once back at the cabin, Abby went inside to change into riding clothes while Gideon saddled Buck and Snuggles. Abby's horse was a fine animal and Gideon liked to ride him on occasion, but he never called the horse by name. He considered castration humiliating enough without adding to the horse's burden with such an effeminate name.

As Abby walked out of the cabin, she sashayed towards Gideon in her riding britches and a white frilly blouse under a jacket. She loved wearing the britches and Gideon loved seeing her in them. Some men thought it blasphemous for a woman to wear pants, but not him. Whenever she wore them, he made a point to walk a step behind her just to watch her butt wiggle.

"You're looking mighty fine," Gideon said as he handed the reins of Snuggles to his wife.

With mock humility, Abby said, "You mean these old things?"

"We better ride before I lose my willpower."

Climbing onto her horse, Abby said, "If I wanted, I could control you like a grinder's monkey."

"I just might let you," Gideon said as he heeled Buck into moving.

Drenched in bright sunlight, the day looked beautiful but chilly, and made the horses frisky. Putting the animals into a lope to take off their edge, the couple headed to the outpost shack where String Callow would take up residence. They found String chopping firewood in front of the cabin.

"Hello," String called out as Gideon and Abby rode into the yard.

"How are things coming along?" Abby asked.

"I about got the place fixed to my satisfaction, but I believe I should have negotiated for furnished firewood," String announced in his offhand manner.

"Good luck with that. I hate chopping my own and I sure wouldn't do it for anybody else," Gideon said as he climbed off Buck and shook String's hand.

"Ma'am, I was hoping that we could ride out to look the herd over tomorrow to start coming up with a plan for the ranch," String said.

"Please call me Abby. There's no need for that ma'am business. Meeting up tomorrow sounds like a good idea. Ride over to our cabin whenever you want Monday and we'll look over the herd."

"I looked at your cattle yesterday. You have some good beef. I think with a little culling, and maybe a new bull, we can have a fine herd."

"We'll let you get back to chopping. We just wanted to stop in and check on you," Abby said.

"Have a nice day," String said before the couple rode away.

"Where to now?" Gideon asked.

"You know where. We always have to stop at the aspen grove," Abby answered before taking off in a lope and leaving behind Gideon.

Gideon contemplated racing his wife, but thought better of the idea. Snuggles was a younger horse than Buck, and as much as Gideon hated to admit it, his mount had begun to lose some of his speed. Putting the gelding into an easy lope, Gideon contented himself with following his wife to the grove.

The grove sat on a hill on the original Johann homestead and had served as the favorite picnic spot for the couple back in their teenage years. Joann had been conceived there on such an occasion. And after Gideon's return to Last Stand, the place had served as the location for Abby to tell him that she planned to divorce Marcus.

Abby already sat on what she called their rock by the time Gideon rode up.

Patting the rock, she said, "Hurry up, old man."

Gideon climbed up onto the rock. "Well, at least our rock hasn't weathered away."

"I know. That's what I love about this spot. No matter what happens in our life, this place remains unchanged. I take some comfort in that," Abby said as she pulled her jacket closed.

"Do you think things will ever get back to normal?"

"Sure they will. It will be a new normal, but still normal. Losing Tess has changed all of us. I know her death haunts you, but we'll come to terms with it. We have to, but those kinds of losses take a while. I think even Joann will eventually make peace with herself. I just don't know if she'll ever come back here and be

Zack's wife. That girl is a little too independent for her own good and has a little too much of you in her. But Gideon, you and I have lived through too much not to appreciate what we have now. We will be happy," Abby said, leaning against Gideon.

Wrapping his arm around his wife, Gideon snickered and said, "I know what will make me happy."

"Good God, you are as horny as a teenager. You're going to have to wait until we get home. There's no way you are sweet-talking me out of my clothes out here. It's too chilly," Abby chided.

"I know. I'm content just to sit here for a while. I love the children, but it sure is nice to be away from them. We don't get to hear the quiet very often."

"Shh," Abby said before giving Gideon a kiss.

Chapter 19

First thing Monday morning, Gideon met with District Attorney Kile.   The two men had a good working relationship and got right down to business. Gideon did his best to cajole D.A. Kile into coming up with every charge imaginable against Lewis Wise, including the murder of Julen Laxalt.   The district attorney had laughed and reminded Gideon that the sheriff had failed to provide nary a single shred of evidence to classify Julen's death as murder.   But Kile did realize that he needed to help Gideon bring pressure against the rancher to prevent an all-out war. He agreed to take liberties with some of the lesser charges that he probably wouldn't have a chance in hell of winning in court.   With the charges agreed upon, the two men shook hands and Gideon walked to the jail.

At his office, Gideon grabbed a map of the county and put on his heavy coat. The temperature had plunged during the night and the sky look a menacing gray with occasional flurries of snow coming down.

"Do you want me to go see Lewis with you?" Finnie asked.

"Nah, there's no need for both of us freezing off our asses," Gideon answered.

"You seem to have a spring in your step today."

The statement actually caused Gideon to stop mid-step and turn towards Finnie. "What's that supposed to mean?"

"Oh, nothing. You just seem to be in a good mood today," Finnie said offhandedly.

With annoyance in his voice, Gideon asked, "Is this in reference to the fact that you saw Sarah take the kids home with her yesterday?'

Grinning, Finnie said, "I did notice that. Did you and Abby have a fine day?"

Shaking his head, Gideon said, "One of these days you're going to be one of those old men that forces hugs on pretty young girls and makes them want to vomit from that old man smell."

"And you're going to be so sensitive that no one will be able to have a conversation with you without you getting your drawers in a wad," Finnie said just before Gideon disappeared out the door.

Gideon rode to Lewis Wise's ranch and knocked on the door to the home. Mrs. Wise greeted Gideon and led him to the bedroom where Lewis lay stretched out under the covers in bed. The sheriff noticed that Lewis wore a work shirt and that a pair of boots by the bed had moisture on the toes.

"How are you feeling, Lewis?" Gideon asked.

"You liked to have killed me, Gideon. I've been in bed ever since I got back from seeing Doc Abram," Lewis said.

"Knock it off, Lewis. I can see where you've worn your boots outside this morning. D.A. Kile and I came up with eight charges against you including inciting a riot and destruction of personal property. You could spend at least five years in prison, so you best listen. I came up with a line through Black Cat Mountain running east to west. Anything north of the line would be for the sheepherders and everything south will be for the ranchers. You ranchers are getting the best of the land by a longshot. I still have to get the sheepherders to agree to it, too. You have three days to decide whether you want to agree to the deal or would rather face the charges. You have to get all the other ranchers on board with this also. I also sent a telegram to U.S. Marshal Wilcox informing him that I may need reinforcements," Gideon said.

"You think you got everything the way you want it, don't you? Even if I agree, I don't know that I have much sway with the other ranchers."

"You're the one that stirred everybody up and you will be the one to calm them back down."

"There are two or three ranches up that way that use the land you're talking about for grazing. I don't imagine they will be too thrilled with your proposal," Lewis said.

"Well, we could make the boundary everything south of your original homestead. I'm sure the sheepherders would love that land," Gideon said.

Lewis climbed out of bed and moved towards the sheriff. "All right, you made your point. I'll see what I can do. Those damn sheep will be the ruin of this county – mark my words. And they're liable be the ruin to your job."

"That may be, but I'll be damn if I'll sit back and watch you railroad those sheepherders and get people killed. Lewis you are better than this. I would think that the death of Julen Laxalt would sit heavy on your mind. That young man probably wasn't a whole lot different than your father when he moved here."

"My father came with beef, not sheep. That's a different class of man completely," Lewis said before looking down at his feet. "I'll come to town and let you know where things stand."

Gideon headed north to find the sheepherders. The wind blew out of the west and the snow came down at an angle in big fluffy flakes. Ever since he'd been old enough to sit on a horse, he had enjoyed riding in a snowfall. He buttoned up his coat and pulled on his gloves, relaxing as he rode. To his way of thinking, there were a lot worse things in life than taking a horse ride in the snow through the mountains.

The Laxalt brothers were sitting around a fire eating lunch when Gideon found them. Dominique offered the sheriff some of their meal, but Gideon didn't recognize the food or like its smell and politely declined. Gideon pointed out Black Cat Mountain to the south and then its location on the map before explaining the proposal.

Dominque looked at Gideon and said, "There will be no justice for my brother, will there?"

Gideon glanced down at the map and then back at Dominque. "I don't think so. I believe there are six men that know what happened and unless one of them has a reason to talk, I have no evidence," he said.

"Julen deserved better."

"Yes, he did and if I could make them talk I would, but those ranchers will stick together until the end. Nothing that happened the other day is enough to break their silence."

"Very well. We will agree to the proposal. It is fair to us and better than dying. Our mother could not take losing another son."

Not wishing to smell the brothers' pungent food a moment longer, Gideon shook each one of the men's hands and departed to find the Mexican.

A good four inches of snow now covered the ground and made Buck act like a young colt. He nearly threw

Gideon when he unexpectedly kicked his rear legs into the air. Gideon had to grab the saddle horn to keep from flying over the horse's head. He grinned at the animal's spunk even as he felt embarrassed for grabbing the saddle to stay on board.

Sid greeted Gideon as if they were friends now and headed towards the tent without prompting.

"Did you tell those ranchers that I shot their horses out from under them?" Sid asked.

"No, I made them think that I did it. I didn't see a reason to make them hate your bunch worse than they do now. Besides, it never hurts when people think their sheriff is a hell of a shot," Gideon said.

Chuckling, Sid said, "I suppose you have a point."

The weather had forced Antonio Cortez into his tent. The Mexican sat bundled in a sheepskin coat, looking miserable.

"I was not bred for this type of weather, senor," Antonio said when Sid led Gideon into the tent.

"This is nothing. You are in for a long winter if you think this is cold," Gideon said as he took a seat.

"So I fear. Let's have some tequila to knock off the chill," Antonio said and motioned with his head for Sid to retrieve the liquor.

"You're going to spoil me," Gideon said after taking his first sip of the drink.

"I appreciate your effort to keep the peace. That has not always been the case in my travels. You are an honorable man."

Gideon looked over at Antonio and realized that the Mexican liked him. The idea seemed surprising and he wasn't sure if a friendship with Antonio was a good thing. He still had some doubts about the Mexican's character. "Thank you," he said before going on to explain the proposal that he had already made twice that day.

Antonio took a sip of his drink and looked at the sheriff. "You know, my men and I could hold our own against twenty, maybe twenty-five, of those cowboys."

"I know. I fought in a war, too. Your men are professionals and those ranchers aren't. But the thing is, if you do that, they'll go hire ten professionals and there will be one hell of a bloodbath. It's hard running a sheep empire if you are dead," Gideon said.

Antonio chuckled before tipping his glass and finishing off his drink. "So very true. So very true. I can live with the agreement as long as the ranchers honor it, but if they don't, I will make them pay dearly."

"How about one more drink. We'll toast to peace."

Grinning, Antonio poured another drink for each of them. The two men clinked their glasses together and downed the liquor.

"I look forward to your next visit," Antonio said as Gideon arose.

"Stay warm," Gideon said before leaving the tent.

For the first time since the trouble with the sheepherders had begun, Gideon felt hopeful that there might be a peaceful resolution to the problem. He headed home, arriving just as Abby finished cooking supper.

During the meal, he listened to his wife talk excitedly about all the plans for the herd that she and String had discussed that day. He hadn't seen Abby this excited in a long time. She and String planned to purchase better quality bulls and take a hard eye to culling the cows. Gideon could hardly get a word in edgewise. Instead, he enjoyed the tasty meal and smiled at his new ranch baron.

Chapter 20

After a week of being cooped up in the house taking care of Zack, Joann decided to spend the day helping her father tend to the herd. A big winter storm looked to be moving in and they planned to move the herd farther down into a valley for protection against the elements. Joann had risen early and left with her poppa before Zack had awakened that morning.

Zack looked up in surprise when Rita brought him his breakfast. He scooted himself into a reclining position and attempted to smile at his mother-in-law through the pain of moving his body.

"Did Joann finally tire of nursing me?" Zack asked.

"I think it was more of a bad case of cabin fever," Rita answered as she looked Zack over to determine his condition. His head was healing nicely though he looked ridiculous with the chunk of hair cut away. He appeared pale, and under his eyes looked dark. Still, all in all, considering the condition he had arrived in, he looked remarkably resilient.

"I can understand that. I'd get out of this room too if I could walk."

"Just count your blessings that you're alive. You'll be good as new before long," she said as she placed a tray of food onto Zack's lap.

Taking a sip of coffee and then a bite of egg, Zack asked, "I'm never going to get her back, am I?"

Rita pulled the chair over to the bed and sat down on it. "I don't know, Zack. She's my daughter, and still half the time I don't have a clue on what goes on in Joann's head. She has herself convinced that she can live here like an old maid and be content. Once she gets a hold on something, she is like a dog with a bone."

"Would you like us to get back together?"

"Of course, I take marriage vows very seriously. And besides, you two are so good together. A lot of men wouldn't put up with Joann's nonsense. Her poppa and I spoiled that girl too much."

Zack grinned and took a bite of bacon. "I don't know. Before we lost Tess, Joann sure kept things lively. I certainly was never bored in her company."

"I would say not. She always kept things stirred up around here too."

"How can I win her back?" Zack asked.

Rita patted the bun at the back of her head while she thought about the question. "You just need to be yourself and appear strong. You know how she hates weakness or whining. Don't even think of asking her to go back to Colorado with you. And don't baby her. She needs to remember what she had and what she's leaving behind. Things need to be as normal between you two as possible considering the circumstances. Once you've healed, I don't believe you'll ever get another chance."

"Thank you. You've made a lot of sense and I'll try my best. Finally standing up to Joann is how I won her over in the first place. Maybe I should have put my foot down more after Tess died, but Joann was so pathetic. I just wasn't much good at being tough."

"That's a fine line for sure. You need to take your laudanum now. The doctor says you need lots of rest to heal and you can't rest if you're in pain."

"I hate taking that stuff. It makes me feel as if I'm in a fog. Do you think this pain in my pelvis will get better?"

Rita grabbed the bottle of medicine and poured a tablespoon before feeding it to Zack. "The doctor thinks you will heal just fine. He is an arrogant cuss, but he knows his medicine. You have to get well. I can't afford to feed you forever," Rita said and smiled at Zack. "Just so you know, I don't think Joann could have picked a better man than you. Now get some rest."

∞

Joann brought Zack his supper. He snored softly as she entered the room and provided her the opportunity to size up her husband's condition. Seeing Zack in such a weakened state, Joann could feel herself trying to slip back into a dark place that she never wanted to go again. Zack looked so young and helpless that he didn't seem old enough to be the man that she had married. She still had trouble sleeping at night for fear that he might die before morning's light.

Zack opened his eyes and squinted to make them focus. "Good God – the way you dress," he said at seeing his wife's outfit of men's trousers with suspenders and a work shirt and her hair pinned up tightly against her scalp. "You look like a fourteen year old boy."

Pulling her shoulders back, Joann straightened her posture and held the tray stiffly. "The way I dress works just fine for a ranch. It's not as if I'm trying to impress anybody out here anyway. Here I was worrying and feeling sorry for you and then you have to open your mouth. You never could say the right thing if your life depended on it," she said as she waited for Zack to sit up.

Wincing as he moved, Zack said, "All right, I'm ready."

Seeing the pain in his face, Joann's tone softened and she said, "Does it hurt a lot?"

"I'm fine. A bullet isn't any worse than your words," he said as Joann placed the tray in his lap.

"You weren't being exactly nice either," she said defensively.

"I suppose not, but it pains me to see you dressed like that. You're too pretty of a girl to hide it under men's clothing. You always looked so good in a dress."

Grinning, Joann leaned forward and whispered, "I thought you always liked me best naked."

Zack giggled before scrunching his face in pain from the exertion. Shocked that Joann had said something intimate, his mind raced for a suitable reply. "A lot of good it would do me now. Just the thought is liable to tear my wound open and let me bleed to death."

"I was always too much for you anyways," Joann teased.

"That's not how I remember things. I don't remember either of us having anything to complain about."

Turning serious, Joann asked, "Is anybody watching over the homestead?"

"Gideon and Ethan are taking turns checking on the place. I hope that no squatters will move into the cabin. Gideon would take care of them I would imagine."

"Did you check on Tess's grave before you came up here?"

"I visited her before I left. Everything looked fine."

"I hate the thought of her being out there with the cold coming."

"Joann, Tess is in Heaven now. She's in a good place and doing fine."

"I know, but it gets so cold," Joann said as she quickly flicked a tear away. "Get to eating before your food gets cold."

Chapter 21

Gideon and Finnie arrived early at the town hall for a meeting with the ranchers, Dominique Laxalt, and Antonio Cortez. Earlier in the week, Lewis Wise came to town and informed the sheriff that he had gotten area ranchers, including those to the north, to agree to the land sharing proposal. Though the document wasn't legally binding, Gideon had nonetheless insisted that the sheepherders and some prominent ranchers sign the proposal.

Dominique arrived first and Antonio a short time later. Through the window, Gideon could see the other Laxalt brothers standing nervously outside with their shotguns. Three of Antonio's guards also stood on the boardwalk. The six ranchers arrived together by horseback and entered the building as if they owned the place. Lewis Wise carried a box of cigars that Gideon assumed to be a token of goodwill to smoke after the signing.

Lewis made a show of passing cigars to the lawmen and the ranchers while skipping the sheepherders. "Light up, boys, so we don't have to smell that sheep shit," he said as he sat back down in his chair.

Gideon had a hard time believing what he just saw. Lewis Wise was the last person in the room that needed to be making trouble. Clenching his fists, Gideon could feel his pulse in his temples. He inhaled loudly through his nose before blowing out his breath and standing. Lewis sat in the middle of the ranchers looking smug while grinning at the others. Gideon walked behind the ranchers and grabbed Lewis by the collar, flipping the rancher and his chair onto the floor. With his fist, Gideon smashed the cigar box and tossed a couple of the stogies to Dominique and Antonio.

"Lewis, you have tried my patience about as far as it will go. Now get your ass up and don't cause any more trouble," Gideon said before walking around the table and making a point of lighting the sheepherders' cigars.

All eyes were on the sheriff now and he waited for one of the ranchers to run his mouth, but nobody said a word. After Lewis reseated himself, Gideon motioned for Finnie to pass out a copy of the agreement for each man to read. Antonio, in a show of compassion that Gideon wouldn't have expected from the aristocratic Mexican, read the document aloud to Dominique.

After waiting for the men to finish reading, Gideon asked, "Does anybody have anything to say before signing?"

"I do," Antonio said before taking a puff on the cigar. "Every rancher I have ever met has made a point to make sure I understand that they were the ones that settled this land and fought off the Indians and everything else. I look at the six of you and I see nothing but cowards. You didn't have the balls to take on my men and me. Instead, you attacked this nearly defenseless man and his brothers twice. You killed his brother and then hide behind each other so that no one has to pay for his crime. If anyone bothers them again, I will take matters into my own hands. Now I will sign this agreement for the sake of peace, but I find you all disgusting."

"Mighty big talk for a greaser," Lewis said.

Standing, Gideon said, "Gentlemen, nobody has to like each other here. As long as everybody signs the agreement and sticks to it, we can all coexist without trouble. If a war breaks out, some of you sitting at this table will surely die. Just sign the damn thing and stay out of each other's hair."

Antonio signed the document and Dominique made his mark. The ranchers all looked at each other until Carter Mason signed his name. As they passed the documents around, every man signed all eight copies. By the time they finished, the smoke from ten men puffing on cigars hung so thick that breathing proved nearly impossible. Everyone made a quick exit outside.

"Sheriff, I'm going to do my damnedest to make sure you don't get reelected," Lewis said before mounting his horse.

"Have at it, Lewis. I still might solve Julen's murder in the meantime," Gideon said.

As all of the men departed, Finnie said, "That Cortez fellow might be all right afterall. I've never trusted a Mexican before."

"Maybe. I sure wouldn't want to cross him though. Let's go get Doc and have a beer. I need to listen to him grouse a little to get my mind on something else."

"Just a moment," Finnie said before running back into the hall. He returned with his pocket bulging with the remaining cigars. "Lewis has expensive taste and there's no need to waste some fine smokes."

Doc gladly accepted the invitation. The cold front that had moved in earlier in the week had settled in and made walking outside miserable. Doc covered his mouth with his scarf and pulled his hat low to fend off the spitting snow as they walked to the Last Chance.

Delta brought the three men their beers before hurrying away to another table.

"Where's Mary?" Doc asked as he looked around the saloon.

"She should be in directly. She wanted to spend some time with Sam today," Finnie answered.

"Sam. Now that's a good strong name. That child might grow up to be a doctor or maybe even a president," Doc said.

"When you die just remember to leave your namesake some of that stash you've been hoarding your whole life," Finnie said.

"With a mother that is as astute at business as Mary, that child will have plenty of inheritance. Thank goodness Sam won't have to depend on you," Doc said before taking a drink.

"You probably won't die anyways. You'll just petrify and keep on yapping," Finnie said.

Mary walked into the saloon. She smiled at seeing the men sitting at the table and walked over to join them. Finnie jumped up and pulled out a chair for his wife, winking at Doc as he did so.

"So did you get everyone to sign your agreement?" Mary asked.

"We did. It wasn't a pleasant affair," Gideon said before taking a swallow of beer.

"Do you think it will hold?" she asked.

"I think so as long as Lewis Wise behaves himself. He's the ringleader and troublemaker. I think Carter Mason regrets ever getting involved in the whole mess. He had a hard time looking me in the eye," Gideon said.

Doc took a sip of beer and set down his glass. "Enough about that. I still can't find anybody wanting to come into my practice. Those grandchildren are liable to be grown before I ever get to see them again. And if I up and die, Last Stand will be in a fix."

"They'll probably shut the town down and everybody will up and move away if that happens," Finnie said sarcastically.

Mary patted Doc's hand. "Don't talk of dying. I'm sure you'll find someone eventually. And I bet John and his family come back next spring or summer. They loved Last Stand and seeing you. I know you'll find somebody come spring."

"I suppose, but it's not even winter yet. Those grandkids made me soft," Doc said.

"Your reputation for being the grouchiest doctor west of the Mississippi has probably made you a legend even back east," Finnie said.

Doc shook his head at the Irishman, but failed to come up with a rebuttal.

Turning towards Gideon, Mary said, "Have you heard from Zack? I haven't heard you say anything about him lately.

"No, not a word since he reached his aunt's house. I'm getting worried about him. I think I'm going to send a telegram to Abby's aunt and see if he's there. I didn't want to let the cat out of the bag that he's coming, but I'm getting concerned."

"I bet when you found that boy on the trail you never guessed he'd be such a big part of your life," Mary said.

"You know, I've thought about that lots of times – how a chance meeting can make such a profound change in your life. I didn't even know Joann when I found Zack and now I go to bed every night worrying about the both of them. I certainly never imagined him being my son-in-law or that I'd get the opportunity to be so close to Joann," Gideon said.

"That's kind of how I feel about that drunk little Irishman you brought to town," Mary said and giggled.

Holding his beer mug up as if making a toast, Finnie said, "Oh, Mary, chance had nothing to do with us being together. You never had a prayer in the world – you were as destined to fall for my Irish charm as surely as an apple is to the ground. It is both a gift and a burden." Finnie took a big swig of beer as the others laughed at the Irishman.

Chapter 22

Once the men finished their beer, Mary ran Gideon, Finnie, and Doc out of the Last Chance, telling them in no uncertain terms that she had work to do and they were interfering. Stepping outside, the cold air hit the men's faces like bathing in ice water. A steady snow floated to the ground and had already accumulated a couple of inches deep. The heavy air sank the smoke from all the fireplaces raging in the town and made the street appear as if in a fog. Doc walked back to his office while Gideon and Finnie headed to the jail.

"You better head on home," Finnie said.

"I told Abby I planned to stay in town tonight to watch the Pearl West," Gideon said.

"I can go over there. It's not payday and with the cold, I doubt there will be much business anyways. I'm sure Abby doesn't appreciate keeping the fire going all night by herself."

"I don't want you over there. If something were to happen, Cyrus would claim that you acted out of interest for the Last Chance. Most people would know the truth, but we don't need a stink. The ranchers are mad enough at us right now as it is. And Abby will be fine for one night."

"Cyrus has really gotten under your skin, hasn't he? Since business is not doing as well as he expected, maybe he will move on."

"I don't like him, that's for sure, but I doubt Cyrus ever leaves a town until the law is about ready to throw his sorry ass in jail and we aren't close to that," Gideon said.

"I'm going to head on home and spend some time with Sam, but I'll be in the Last Chance later tonight if you need me," Finnie said.

"Go on. I hope I have no need to see you until the morning," Gideon said. "Oh, by the way, give me a couple of those cigars. I don't have anything else to do until later and I don't have much of an appetite."

Reluctantly pulling two stogies from his pocket, Finnie handed them to Gideon. "Just as it always is. We Irish do all the dirty work and you German types get all the spoils," he said before stepping outside.

Finnie had only taken a few steps when he heard someone call, "Mr. Ford, may I have a moment of your time."

Turning towards the sound of the voice, Finnie saw Cyrus Capello walking towards him.

"What can I do for you?" Finnie asked skeptically.

"It's too cold out here to talk. Please walk down to the Pearl West with me. I only want a moment of your time," Cyrus said.

"Very well," Finnie said and followed Cyrus down and across the street into the saloon.

Cyrus led Finnie into his office and shut the door. "Can I offer you a drink?"

"No, I'm good. What can I do for you?" Finnie repeated.

"I'm sure your wife told you that I offered to buy the Last Chance. I'm asking you to reconsider. I'll pay you twice what it is worth."

"Mary already told you that she doesn't want to sell. The Last Chance is her pride and joy," Finnie said, trying to sound amiable.

"But you're the man of the house and I thought you wouldn't pass up such an attractive offer. Your restaurant is doing well and you could concentrate on running it."

"Mary owns the saloon, not me. She's not going to sell," Finnie said with finality.

"Even if I made a ridiculously generous offer?"

Finnie shook his head.

"I should have known a paddy would let a woman lead him around by the nose. I'm surprised any of you have the balls to procreate," Cyrus yelled.

"And just like a damn dago to think he can buy whatever he wants and everybody is supposed to stand to the side," Finnie yelled back.

"You'll come to rue this day. I'll have your damn saloon yet," Cyrus hollered.

Taking a deep breath, Finnie said in his calmest voice, "You don't want to mess with me. If something were to happen, I'd kill you without a thought."

Standing, Finnie calmly opened the door and walked out of the saloon.

∞

Turning the wick up in the oil lamp, Gideon pulled the book he had ordered from the general store out of the drawer. The tome was a collection of Shakespeare's works. His mother had gotten him interested in the bard's writing when Gideon was a teenager, but he hadn't read any of the prose since leaving for the war.

He had bought the book for nights when he couldn't sleep. After lighting up one of Finnie's stogies, he began reading. His skills at interpreting the verse had badly eroded and he found himself rereading each passage numerous times before comprehending the meaning. He didn't find the effort frustrating, but rather a challenge that he hoped to master.

After a couple of hours of smoking cigars and striving to read, Gideon put the book away and walked outside. The cloud cover and snow blocked out any light from the moon or stars. Only the streetlamps provided any illumination as he walked to the Pearl West. Inside the saloon, Gideon found no more than a dozen cowboys. At one table, four men played a game of poker, but the craps and Faro tables sat empty. Gideon walked to the bar and ordered a beer.

The bartender scurried to the back and reemerged with Cyrus.

From behind the bar, Cyrus said, "I didn't think maybe the honorable sheriff would set foot back into my humble establishment."

"It's not my preferred choice for sure, but until I'm sure this place runs clean games, you can count on me making visits," Gideon said and took a swig of beer.

"I've come across sheriffs like you before. You think you're so much more damn honest than the rest of us. You're not. You just have a different set of priorities in which you'd be willing to be underhanded," Cyrus said.

"Yes, I'd have no problems with breaking the law to uphold it," Gideon said and stared at Cyrus.

"Is that a threat?"

"Leave Mary alone. You don't want to go there."

"It's not a crime to see if somebody would want to sell their business. I did it in a spirit of friendliness. You seem very attached to Mrs. Ford. Perhaps she's more than just a friend. I'm sure it wouldn't be hard to pull the wool over the eyes of that stupid Irishman," Cyrus said.

Gideon stared at Cyrus and contemplated smashing his Colt upside the saloonkeeper's head, but decided against showing how badly the words had gotten under his skin. "Why don't you shut the hell up and let me drink my beer in peace. I didn't know the price included a lecture from the saloonkeeper."

Somebody stuck his head in the front door of the Pearl West and yelled, "House fire a couple of blocks behind the Last Chance."

Shoving a cowboy out of his way, Gideon was the first out the door. He took off in a run in the direction of the Last Chance. His boots made for poor traction in the deepening snow and he slipped and nearly fell as he ran. As he ran down the side street between the jail and saloon, Gideon saw the flames shooting out of the old Clary house.

The home had sat empty for a couple of years before a milliner from Pennsylvania named Lyman Dozier and his family had moved into the house in the early fall. The two-story structure had smoke billowing and flames shooting out of most of the windows. News of the fire must have reached the Last Chance well before making its way to the Pearl West. A bucket brigade had already formed to douse the fire and a ladder rested against the one upstairs window with no fire darting out of it.

Gideon spotted Mayor Howard and grabbed him. "Did somebody go up that ladder?" he asked.

"We could hear a child screaming and Finnie went up. We tried, but couldn't stop him," Hiram answered.

"Damn it to hell. How long has he been up there?"

"Maybe a couple of minutes."

"Somebody get Doc," Gideon said as he started to ascend the ladder.

"Gideon, come back here. You can't do anything now," Hiram yelled.

Out of the corner of his eye, Gideon saw Mary standing in the snow. Both of her hands were pressed against her mouth and she looked like a lost child. He forced the scene from his mind and rapidly climbed the ladder. As he reached the top, the heat hit him like scalding water. He bellowed, "Finnie."

"Gideon, keep yelling. I'll follow your voice. I can't see," Finned called out.

"Finnie, I'm over here. For Christ's sake, get your ass over here right now," Gideon rambled on at the top of his lungs. The wait felt like minutes and the heat and smoke coming from the window seemed too intense for someone to emerge from alive.

Finnie leaned out of the window holding a little girl and coughing violently. Gideon grabbed the child from the Irishman's arm and began descending. Finnie crawled out the window and slid down the ladder as if it were a pole. Smoke wafted off his shirt as he barreled towards the ground. Gideon jumped out of the way to keep from getting knocked over by the rapidly descending Irishman. Still coughing, Finnie plunged into the snow and rolled to cool his searing skin.

Gideon looked down at the little girl. She looked as if she were a sleeping four-year-old. Her blond hair looked singed on the ends and her body felt hot to the touch.

Doc walked up to the sheriff. "Put her in the snow and heap it on her. If she's burned it'll take some of the heat out of it," he said.

As Gideon and Hiram heaped snow onto the child, she opened her eyes and began coughing. She looked at the two strangers and began crying hysterically through her fits of coughs.

Mary knelt beside her husband, stroking his face. Finnie lay with his back in the snow trying to take the heat out of it. The pain had been so intense that he thought he had been on fire as he slid down the ladder.

"Go comfort the child. I'll be fine," Finnie said between bouts of coughs.

Gideon and Hiram had moved back and Doc leaned over the child trying to calm her.

Mary walked up to them. "Can't we get her out of the snow?" she asked.

"Sure," Doc said. "We need to take her to my office."

Mary scooped the child up before Gideon had a chance.

"Hi. My name's Mary. Everything is going to be fine. All right?"

The child nodded her head.

"What's your name?" Mary asked as she walked towards the doctor's office.

"Sylvia," the little girl said and coughed some more.

"Do you hurt anywhere?' Mary coaxed.

"My arm hurts," Sylvia answered.

"Well, Doc will fix you right up. You're a pretty little thing."

Gideon walked over to Finnie. The sheriff's legs felt like butter now that they were back on the ground. He dropped down onto his knees beside the Irishman. In a shaky voice, he asked, "How badly are you hurt?"

Finnie coughed before speaking. "I don't know. My back is burned and my lungs feel seared. Was I on fire?"

"I don't think so, but I'm not sure. I didn't really get a chance to see much."

"It's a good thing you're a loudmouth. I was lost in there and thinking that this was the end until you piped up," Finnie said.

Gideon despised how emotional he'd become in the last few years. For somebody that had gone years without feeling much of anything, these day just about anything got to him. He felt himself growing misty and he reached down to grab Finnie's arm. "That might have been the bravest thing I've ever seen anybody do," he said, his voice almost breaking.

"Thanks. I just thought about Sam and how I couldn't bear to lose him. I sure didn't want somebody else to lose their child. I guess she's the only one that made it out though."

"I think so. We better get you up and to Doc," Gideon said as he pulled on Finnie's arm.

The house popped and cracked as the second floor collapsed into a fireball and sent flames shooting up into the sky. Having given up on saving the place, the volunteers worked to keep the fire from spreading to the next-door houses.

"Hiram, I'll be at Doc's if you need me. I think they got it under control," Gideon called out as he walked away with Finnie.

Once they were inside the doctor's office, the two lawmen found Doc and Mary huddled around the little girl. They had stripped her of her clothes and Doc gently applying salve to the child's right arm.

"How is she?" Finnie asked.

"A lot better than if you hadn't rescued her," Doc said. "She has some blisters on one arm and I need to listen to her lungs. How are you?"

"I'll let you tell me," Finnie said before deciding that he should remove his shirt in case it might start sticking to his skin.

"Take a big breath for me," Doc instructed the child and demonstrated what he wanted from her as he placed the stethoscope against her chest.

Sylvia did as asked and coughed from inhaling deeply.

"Does that hurt?" Doc asked the child.

"A little," Sylvia answered.

The doctor continued listening as Sylvia inhaled deep breaths and occasionally coughed. Pulling the stethoscope out of his ears, Doc said, "She doesn't sound too bad. We'll know more in a day or two. Lungs can be a tricky subject. Mary, would you wrap her in a blanket and hold her while I check Finnie? Watch her arm."

"Where are Momma and Poppa and Dougie?" Sylvia asked.

"They can't be here with you right now. You'll be safe with me," Mary said as she wrapped the child in a blanket.

As Finnie walked to the table, Mary got a view of her husband's back.

"Finnie, you're hurt," Mary cried out.

Lying down on his belly, Finnie dangled his arms over the sides of the table as the doctor looked on. The back of Finnie's shoulders were covered in blisters and oozed clear fluid. The doctor grabbed a bottle of vinegar and began swathing the wounds.

"It's not as bad as it looks. This will heal just fine," Doc said as he looked over at Mary.

After finishing with the vinegar, Doc retrieved the jar of salve and began applying the thick grease.

"Good God, your calloused hands feel like you're gouging me with sticks," Finnie called out.

Doc opened his mouth to call Finnie a baby and then caught himself. He wasn't going to insult the Irishman on the night he had risked his life to save a child he didn't even know. "I'll try to be gentler," he said instead.

Surprised at Doc's response, Finnie looked over his shoulder at the doctor. "I must be dying if you're being nice."

"Are you burned anywhere else?"

"I don't think so."

"Sit up and let me check your chest," Doc commanded.

The doctor attentively listened to Finnie's lungs. "How much does it hurt to breathe?"

"Some. It kind of feels like a bad chest cold, but burns a little."

"I think you'll be fine, but we'll have to wait to see for sure. I want you to take deep breaths as much as possible. That'll help keep your lungs clear," Doc instructed.

"I've had quite the day," Finnie said. "When I left the jail that dago flagged me down and tried to buy the saloon and now the fire. I don't know which proved worse."

"He tried again?" Gideon asked.

"He got all mouthy when I told him Mary wouldn't sell," Finnie said.

Gideon shook his head.

Mary stood up and handed the child to Gideon. She walked over to Finnie and wrapped her hands around his head while placing her cheek next to his. All of her stoicism gave way and she started to cry. "I've never been so proud of you or loved you more, but if you would've died I would have still been giving you hell when we met again," she said and laughed through her sobs.

Doc washed his hands before turning towards Finnie and Mary. "Mary, you and Sylvia can sleep in the spare room. I want you to make Sylvia take deep breaths when you can. Finnie can sleep in my room. I'll sleep in the chair. I don't want either one of them going back out in the cold air."

"We're going to have to name another kid after Doc for sure now," Finnie said.

The doctor gave Finnie an irritated look, but didn't respond.

"What about Sam? He'll need fed," Mary said, realizing that Mrs. Penny probably wondered why neither she nor Finnie had relieved her of the baby.

Gideon held up his hand as if he were a student waiting to be called on by the teacher. "I'll go get him.

Don't worry – I know how to bundle up a baby. I'll have him so swaddled that he'll think summer has arrived."

Chapter 23

Rolling over, Gideon nearly fell off the cot from forgetting that he had slept at the jail. The room looked gray from morning's first light and he decided that he might as well climb on out of the bed into the cold room. Throwing some wood into the stove, he grabbed the bucket to start making the coffee and found a thin coat of ice in the water. He would have loved to go home to the cozy cabin, but knew he'd have to check on Finnie and Sylvia. After that, he needed to look for remains in the fire. If nothing else garnered his attention, he planned to head back to the cabin afterward.

Watching the room gradually brighten with light, Gideon sipped on his coffee and thought about the previous night. The fire had left him mindful once again of how precious life is and how fragile its existence could be. When he had climbed the ladder to the window, dread overcame him to the point that he knew that Finnie was gone. He now considered it nothing short of a miracle that the Irishman had made it out of the house alive. Over the years, Gideon had seen Finnie risk his life on multiple occasions, but he couldn't think of any act braver than crawling into a dark house full of fire and smoke to rescue a child he didn't even know. His mind wandered to Sylvia. The child was now an orphan. He had no idea if she had relatives back east or even what town in Pennsylvania from which the family had come. Somebody would have to care for the child until he figured out what to do with her. Draining the last of his second cup of coffee, he figured he could now walk on over to the doctor's office and check on the two patients.

Gideon almost hit Finnie with the door as he walked into the doctor's office. The Irishman paced the floor in pain. He remained shirtless with the top of his back covered in angry red blisters that oozed fluid. Doc had Sylvia sitting on the table as he listened to her lungs. The child cried loudly for her momma, interrupted by fits of coughing, making it difficult for the doctor to hear. Doc looked as if his patience could be wearing thin. Topping it off, Gideon could hear Sam crying in the back and assumed that Mary was attempting to feed the baby.

"How are you feeling?" Gideon asked Finnie.

"My back feels as if I have a red hot brand against the skin. I can't be still, but my lungs feel better than I feared they would," Finnie answered.

Doc gave Gideon and Finnie an annoyed glare that looked like a teacher threatening that he had better not have to come over to them.

"Gideon, get over here and talk to Sylvia. Mary's feeding the baby and I'm not having any luck," Doc ordered.

"I want my momma," Sylvia said as Gideon walked over.

"I know you do, honey, but you have to stay here while Doc makes you well. I need for you to quit crying. How old are you?" Gideon asked in a soothing voice.

Sylvia held up four fingers.

"Good. Back before you moved here do you remember the town that you lived in?"

Thinking for a moment, Sylvia said, "I don't remember."

"That's all right. Do you remember having a grandpa or grandma or maybe aunts and uncles and cousins?" Gideon further inquired.

Sylvia's expression went blank and Gideon wasn't sure if she didn't understand the question or couldn't recall. She began coughing fiercely.

"We'll try to remember later. Now take deep breaths like you did last night so Doc can listen."

The doctor listened to the child's lungs. His expression gave away his concerns as he moved the stethoscope around Sylvia's chest. "She has some fluid on her lungs," he announced.

Mary came out from the back holding Sam. Sylvia, upon seeing Mary, held out her arms and started crying again. With Sam in one arm, Mary picked up Sylvia with the other and tried to comfort the child.

Doc motioned for Finnie to lie on the table.

Turning to Gideon, Doc said, "You need to go buy that child some clothes and then see if Abby can come help. Mary has her hands full with the baby and everything else. They need to go home and Finnie needs to rest for a few days."

"I have some things that need done at the fire," Gideon said.

"Get Blackie to do it. He's as dependable as they come and can certainly handle the job. There's not going to be much to find. Now go get some clothes and then bring me Abby," Doc ordered.

Gideon tried to size up the child before walking to the dry goods store. There wasn't much of a selection of children's clothing. Most women made their daughter's clothes, but he found a plain dress, some undergarments, and a pair of shoes that he hoped would fit.

On his return to the doctor's office, Gideon stopped at the livery stable and Blackie ambled out to meet the sheriff. Gideon explained the situation and asked the blacksmith to look for the remains with instructions to let the undertaker deal with any that were found. Blackie had been loyal to the sheriff ever since Gideon took the job and gladly agreed to help.

After delivering the clothes, Gideon headed for home. The sun shined as brightly as yesterday had looked ominous. Clumps of snow melted loose from tree branches and fell. One hit Gideon and felt like getting plastered with a mushy snowball from Heaven. He smiled at his metaphor even as some of the snow ran down into the seat of the saddle.

Winnie and Chance were out in the yard making a snowman as Gideon rode into the yard. Sometimes he amazed himself at how much pleasure he derived from seeing their beaming smiles at him. The children had rolled the three pieces of the snowman, and Gideon lifted the chunks into place and helped pack them together. After fetching a bucket, Gideon turned it upside down for Winnie to stand on and told her that she was in charge of making a face.

As Gideon walked into the cabin, he found Abby standing at the window watching.

"You must be Gideon Johann," Abby said a little coolly.

Gideon ignored the jibe and told her of all that had happened.

"That's terrible. I'm sorry for being frivolous. Are Finnie and the little girl going to be all right?"

"I think Finnie will be fine in a few days, but I think Doc is worried about Sylvia's lungs," Gideon answered.

"Sylvia is a pretty name."

"Doc was hoping that you could come relieve Mary. She's got her hands full with Sam, the saloon, and Finnie."

"Gideon, I'd be a bad choice. With Finnie hurt, you won't be able to watch the children, and if Doc thinks that Sam is a distraction, wait until he has Chance running around opening every drawer and breaking vials. You know I would if I could, but that's a bad idea. You need to go tell Sarah. You know she loves taking care of people."

"You think so?" Gideon asked.

Abby gave her husband a look as if he'd gone addlebrained. "Sarah would die for an opportunity to take care of a little girl."

"What if she gets attached?"

"What if she did? Can you think of a better place for that child?" Abby asked.

"What if we find out there's family back east?"

"That may never happen and that child needs somebody to cling to when she realizes her family has perished. It's better that Sarah gets her heart broke than Sylvia not be nurtured. I'm right on this," Abby said with conviction.

"Give me a hug before I go. Doc looked about ready to pop a cork. I better get going," he said as he embraced Abby.

"Are you coming back?"

"I am for a while. I don't know if I'll be able to stay."

"All right, I'll let you get by with it this time," Abby teased. "I'll make you a good meal."

"Thank you. Oh, I about forgot. Do you have any of Winnie's old clothes? Sylvia comes about to here on me," Gideon said as he held his hand to what he thought was the child's height.

"Sure. Come help me with the trunk. I saved them in case I ever had another little girl, but that sure doesn't look to be the case, and I don't know when I'll ever get to be a grandmother again."

Abby found some bedclothes, dresses, and shoes. She kept stopping to reminisce over each outfit and Gideon had to keep prodding her to hurry. They bundled all the things together and Gideon left with them to go see Sarah.

As Gideon rode along, he wondered how well Ethan and Benjamin would take the news of Sarah spending time away from them. He realized that Abby was right and that there would be no stopping Sarah once she heard of Sylvia's plight. Grinning, Gideon chastised himself for worrying about the situation. Ethan Oakes could be a hardheaded man, but when Sarah said to dance the jig, Ethan's feet started flying.

Ethan and Benjamin were splitting and stacking firewood as Gideon rode into the yard.

Setting the axe against the splitting stump, Ethan said, "What do we owe this pleasure?"

"We had a fire in town and I need Sarah's help. Let's go inside and I can tell you all at once," Gideon said as he climbed off Buck and retrieved the bundle of clothes tied to the saddle horn.

"Bad?" Ethan asked.

"Yeah, it was bad. I'd appreciate it if you wouldn't puff up like a toad when you hear what I need. I wouldn't ask if I didn't need her."

Annoyed by the comment, Ethan said, "And what makes you think I'd do that?"

"Because just like me, sometimes you listen as a husband instead of a preacher or in my case a sheriff," Gideon said as he followed Ethan and Benjamin into the cabin.

"Gideon, it's about time you paid me a visit," Sarah said upon seeing the sheriff.

Sarah had nursed Gideon back to health when he returned to Last Stand shot to pieces. During his recovery, she had become his confidante and he loved her like a sister.

"I wish this was only a social visit. That new hatmaker in town, his house burned down last night. Finnie rescued the little girl. They both have some light burns and sore lungs. Doc needs someone to watch over the child at his office. I think he's concerned about her lungs. Mary and Abby have their hands full with the little ones and Finnie will be laid up for a few days. I was hoping that you'd watch her. Her name is Sylvia," Gideon said.

"My goodness, that's terrible. That poor little thing. She must be scared to death. How old is she?" Sarah asked.

"Four," Gideon replied as he watched Ethan and tried to figure out what he was thinking.

"Oh, what a terrible age for her to lose her parents. Old enough to know they're gone and too young to understand it all," Sarah said.

"Sarah, get your things together and I'll hitch the wagon and take you to town. Benjamin and I can survive a few days on my cooking," Ethan said.

"Yes, I have to go. I couldn't bear not helping that child. Is there family anywhere?"

"I don't know yet. I'm going to ask around and see if anybody knows more about the family than I do," Gideon said.

"I better get to packing," Sarah said before flittering away to her and Ethan's bedroom.

"Benjamin, wash up a little. You can ride to town with us," Ethan said before walking outside with Gideon following him.

"That woman loves to nurse the sick," Gideon remarked.

"I'm fine with all this. It's our duty to help the sick and downtrodden, but you know as well as I do that Sarah will fall in love with that little girl. I'll either end up with another child or Sarah will get her heart broken again," Ethan said as they walked to the barn.

"I know, but what would be so bad if you did end up with Sylvia?"

"I don't know. She wouldn't be ours. I might not love her like I should."

"Ethan Oakes, you're so full of crap that those blue eyes are going to turn brown. The first time Sylvia crawls up into your lap, you will be smitten. I'll probably find out that she has family anyway."

"We'll see. I just hope that Sarah doesn't suffer another disappointment. The miscarriages were bad enough."

"I'm going to head back home. Don't forget that bundle of clothes I brought in with me."

"My life was a lot simpler before you showed back up in it," Ethan said.

Gideon grinned and said, "Yeah, but you know you crave the excitement."

Ethan let out a chortle before walking into the barn and watching Gideon ride away.

On the ride to town, Ethan and Benjamin exchanged glances as Sarah rattled on about her concerns for Sylvia. Ethan had known his wife a long time and he wasn't sure he could ever recall her being so consumed with nervous energy. They pulled up in front of the doctor's office and Sarah hurriedly kissed Ethan and Benjamin before hopping off the wagon.

"Be good for your pa. Don't worry, his cooking won't kill you. Love you both. I'll send Gideon to tell you when I can come home," she said as she grabbed her satchel and the bundle of Winnie's clothes.

"We might come pay you a visit and see how things are going," Ethan said.

"Oh, sure," Sarah said as if the idea of Ethan coming back to town had never crossed her mind. She disappeared into the office without looking back.

Once inside, Sarah found Doc restocking his shelves with a shipment of medicine he had received and Mary standing by the table with Sam in her one arm and with her free hand she beat on the back of the little girl. Finnie had walked home shirtless.

"I'm here to help," Sarah announced.

"Thank goodness. I'm exhausted," Mary said.

"Doc, shouldn't you be doing this so Mary could sit down?" Sarah asked.

The doctor spun around and looked at Sarah. Even though he found her comment slightly offensive, he smiled anyway. He had way too much respect for Sarah to be rude. She was one of those good souls where such behavior could never be warranted. "I've taken my turn. I needed to get this medicine put away."

"Hi, honey. My name is Sarah. What's yours?" Sarah asked the child.

"Sylvia."

"You are about the prettiest little thing I've ever laid eyes on. I'm going to watch you so that Miss Mary can go home and rest. All right?"

Sylvia began to cry and then cough. "I want my momma and I don't want Mary to leave."

Leaning in front of the child, Mary said, "Sarah is one of my best friends. She took care of me when I was very sick. She has a son and she knows how to take care of you probably better than me. I promise I'll come back and check on you. All right?"

Sobbing, Sylvia nodded her head.

Mary leaned over and kissed the child's forehead. "I'll see you later," she said before bundling Sam and leaving.

Doc explained to Sarah how to care for Sylvia as he continued to restock his shelves.

"Don't you have anything to give her for her cough?" Sarah asked.

"Actually, we need her to cough up the phlegm. My biggest fear at this point is pneumonia. If we can beat that, I think we'll be fine."

"Well, if I have anything to say about it we will," Sarah said as she placed her arm around Sylvia and pulled the child to her bosom.

Chapter 24

With lunch finished, Jake put on his hat and coat to head to town for his usual Saturday afternoon of card playing. Joann got up from the table and began fixing a plate to take back to the bedroom for Zack. Rita watched her daughter from the table, noticing that the spunk had returned to the way that Joann attacked life. The trait had been sadly lacking since her daughter's return to Wyoming. Joann also wore a dress for a change.

"You seem to be in an awfully good mood today," Rita said.

"What do you mean?" Joann asked.

"I don't know, you just seem light on your feet."

Joann sat back down at the table across from her mother. "Momma, what are you getting at?"

"I guess I'm saying that you have been happier with Zack here than at any time since you returned home."

"I never said that I don't love him, and I was beside myself when I thought he might die, but nothing has changed. I will never put myself in a position to lose another child."

"You're going to break his heart all over again," Rita said.

"That's Zack's fault. He should have never come up here in the first place. There was a reason I didn't answer his letters," Joann said.

"Joann, I'm so sure that you're going to regret this and I don't know why you can't see that you are happier when you are with him. I don't think you'll get another chance with Zack after he leaves."

"That's fine. We can both move on with our lives. I'll always care about Zack, and I do hope he finds happiness again, but I'm not going to change how I feel."

"From the time that you could walk you were the most hardheaded little girl. I had waited so long for a child and was so happy to finally have one that I spoiled you. You've never learned that you're not always right," Rita said.

Standing, Joann said, "Momma, I know you have my best interest at heart, but I'm not a little girl anymore and I'm certainly not going to change now."

Joann finished preparing the plate and walked back to the bedroom. Zack, already sitting up in bed, smiled as his wife walked into the room.

"A man could starve waiting for a meal around here," Zack said.

"It might serve a man right that showed up here uninvited. I thought he had better manners than that," Joann said as she placed the tray in front of Zack.

Zack looked into Joann's eyes trying to decide if the jibe was friendly or not. "At least there are two less highwaymen in the world," he said.

"That's true. Though it would have been preferable not to almost die in the process."

"I'll try to dodge the bullets the next time I'm ambushed. You're certainly feisty and looking pretty today. I can see enough curves in that dress to tell you're a girl," Zack teased.

"Don't you worry about how I'm looking. You're not well enough to be noticing and it wouldn't do you any good even if you were. How are you feeling today?"

"Much better. The pain isn't near as bad as it's been. I'll be glad when I can walk again – I know that. This room is starting to feel as if it's closing in on me."

"That's probably a good thing. Means you're getting better. You'll be able to head back to Colorado in no time."

Zack took a bite of food to end the awkward silence that followed and chewed methodically. "I'm still not sorry that I came up here. I had to see you one more time. At least I went down fighting."

"That you did. Zack, you have to understand that my decision to live here doesn't reflect on how I feel about you. I don't think I would have survived if you had died, but I will not open myself up to the pain that comes with marriage. There'd bound to be more babies and I will not go down that road again. I'd die if I lost another one. Tess was the perfect little baby. She can't be replaced and I can't go there again anyway."

The mention of Tess caused Zack to grimace. He could feel himself sinking as if the loss of the child was pulling him down into an abyss. For the first time, his daughter's death felt like his loss and nobody else's, not even Joann's. At that moment, he realized that he had never truly grieved the loss of his daughter. He had been too numb to mourn the passing at first, and then later, his concern for Joann had taken all of his attention until she moved away. After that, he couldn't really remember what he felt about anything. But now he could feel Tess's death so profoundly that his chest ached. "I miss my Tess," he said before the dam of emotion gave way. Sobs racked his body so hard that he had to gasp for air.

The outburst caught Joann so off guard that she froze. She had never seen Zack so emotional even when Tess had died. He had been her rock and so comforting through the whole ordeal. Thinking back, she realized that she had robbed her husband of the opportunity to grieve. She had been so needy and lost in her own pain that Zack had surrendered his own well-being to care for her.

Joann picked up the tray and set it on the dresser before crawling into bed with Zack and wrapping her arms around him. For the first time since Tess's death, Zack's grief, and not her own, was what mattered to her. She tried to say something comforting, but all the pain, sadness, and guilt got the best of her and she started wailing too. They clung to each other as if each were a raft in a flood and their only means for survival.

Rita heard all the commotion and peeked into the room. She wasn't exactly sure what had happened, but she knew enough to know that some healing had begun. Smiling, she wiped her eyes and scurried back to the kitchen.

Chapter 25

Having promised the family that he would take them to eat at Mary's Place after church on Sunday, Gideon and the family bundled up and headed to town. Abby drove the buckboard wagon with the children and Gideon rode Buck in case he found his services needed in town with Finnie ailing. They intended to check on Sarah and Sylvia after their meal. Only one table remained available as Charlotte seated the family. Families dressed in their Sunday best packed the restaurant. Charlotte stayed on her best behavior for once and surprised Gideon with her natural ease with the children.

After the meal, the family walked towards the doctor's office and saw Ethan and Benjamin's horses tied out front. Inside, they not only found the Oakes family, but Finnie and Mary were also there. Finnie sat on the table as Doc applied salve to his back.

Doc looked over at the new arrivals and said, "Good God, I didn't know this was the town hall. How many more people are going to show up?"

"And if you were here alone, you'd be feeling sorry for yourself that you had no one to talk to. You're never happy unless you're unhappy," Finnie said.

"That sounds like something an Irishman would say. More brawn than brain," Doc said as he slathered more salve onto Finnie's back.

Sylvia interrupted the exchange with a coughing fit that turned everyone's attention towards the child. Sarah sat on a bench patting Sylvia's back as the child rested face down across her lap. Sylvia coughed up phlegm that she spit into a cup that Sarah held.

Sarah appeared exhausted. She looked dark under her eyes and her hair was uncombed and sticking in every direction. Her posture suggested that she didn't have the energy to hold herself erect.

"How is Sylvia doing?" Abby asked the doctor.

"She has pneumonia and a fever. Her arm is healing well, but she's a sick little girl. I can treat the fever, but there's not much I can do about the pneumonia," Doc answered.

Sylvia seemed oblivious to all the commotion around her, never looking towards any of the voices. She wore one of Winnie's nightgowns and her hair looked dirty and greasy, having yet to receive a bath since the fire.

"Sarah, you looked exhausted," Abby noted.

"I'll be fine. I didn't get any sleep, but it's not the first time I've stayed up all night with a sick child."

"This is worse than I somehow imagined. Ethan needs to take you down to the café to get a good meal in you and then you need to go home. I'll watch Sylvia tonight. Gideon is just going to have to watch Chance until you can come back," Abby said.

Gideon glanced at Abby, but didn't say anything. He felt a bit taken aback by her plan, and what it meant for him, but had to admit that her reasoning was sound.

"I have an idea," Mary said. "Mrs. Penny and I can watch over Chance. Winnie can go home with Ethan and Sarah. That'll free Gideon up to do what needs doing, especially since Finnie is useless."

Finnie straightened his posture. "I'm not useless. I'm hurt. I still can't stand clothes on my back," he corrected.

"How are you feeling?" Gideon asked his deputy.

"My lungs are feeling much improved, but these burns will not quit aching. I'm much like Sarah on being light on sleep," Finnie answered.

Sarah began patting her hair into place. "I don't know. My hair's a mess and Sylvia is growing attached to me," she said.

"That's even more reason to do this. She'll really need your attention when she feels better and you don't want to be exhausted or sick," Abby said.

"What do you think, Ethan?" Sarah asked.

"If everybody else is fine with the arrangement, I think it's a good idea," Ethan answered.

Putting the lid back onto the salve, Doc said, "It's settled then. Enough jawing about the subject. Anything to get some of you out of my office."

Sarah leaned down close to Sylvia's face. "I'll be back tomorrow. Abby will watch you tonight," she said.

Sylvia showed no reaction to Sarah's words. She seemed to feel too ill to care about any of that now. Sarah kissed the child's forehead before passing her to Abby. As Sarah walked to the mirror to fix her hair, she swiped tears away from her eyes.

"Ethan, you'll need to take my wagon home with you," Gideon said.

"Thanks, everyone," Ethan said.

"I think we're all in this together," Gideon reminded his friend.

After all the goodbyes were said, and Abby had kissed her children, all took their exit except for Doc, Gideon, Abby, and Sylvia.

Gideon walked over to the doctor and quietly asked, "So how bad is the child?"

"Bad enough, but I've seen a lot worse. My biggest fear is that we've yet to see the worst of this," Doc said.

"I wasn't expecting this. I had bigger concerns for Finnie at the beginning. He seemed worse the night of the fire," Gideon said.

"He probably was at that time, but children don't have the stamina to fight off these kinds of things," Doc answered. "No matter how this all turns out, that was a hell of a brave thing that lunkheaded Irishman did."

Gideon smiled. "That it was and I expect that we'll both be hearing about it for years to come."

Doc rubbed his chin and smiled. "And the worst part is that we won't even be able to give him grief over it."

Walking over to Abby, Gideon sat down beside her.

"I guess we've had a change of plans," he said.

"I had to help Sarah after seeing how things were. I guess in my mind I had all of this a little too sugarcoated."

"Me too."

"She sure is a pretty little thing," Abby said.

"Don't you go getting any ideas," Gideon warned.

"Oh, I'm not. If things work out, I wouldn't think of depriving Sarah of the chance to raise a daughter. I've had my turn and it would be wonderful if Sarah gets hers."

"I need to be going," Gideon said and leaned over and kissed Abby. "I'll see you tomorrow."

Gideon rode to the home of Pastor Roberts. The Methodist preacher had a reputation as a jovial sort. He and Ethan had a running joke about who had saved the most souls on any given week.

Pastor Roberts greeted Gideon at the door. "Gideon, have you come to cross over to the winning side and leave behind Ethan's church?" he said with a smile.

"I would if I could, but some of us have to make a sacrifice for our friends," Gideon said.

"What can I do for you?"

"I understand that the hatmaker, Mr. Dozier, and his family attended your church. I wondered if he ever mentioned any family back east."

"He wasn't much of a talker, but I got the impression that part of the reason they moved here was to get away from family. I think he might have been the first to make something of himself."

"I see."

"Have you checked on Sylvia today? I dropped in yesterday afternoon and she wasn't doing so well," Roberts said.

"She's still not good. Thank you for your time. Always good talking to you," Gideon said.

As Gideon turned to leave, the pastor grabbed Gideon's arm. "You know, Gideon, I think it sure would be a shame to send that little girl back east to an unfortunate situation if we knew she could have a loving home here," the pastor said.

Gideon smiled and rubbed his scar. "Pastor Roberts, I was thinking the same thing. Even if that family had a preacher in it that wasn't on your winning side."

Pastor Roberts let out a chuckle. "Tell Ethan that I said hi when you see him," he said before closing the door.

Chapter 26

Gideon reread the telegram one more time, learning nothing that he hadn't on his first reading. Jake Minder had sent the message informing him that Zack had been shot, was staying with them, and doing well – no other details. The sheriff's mind raced over all the possible scenarios that could have led to his son-in-law getting shot. He even wondered if his daughter had shot her husband in a fit of anger. Joann could be irrational and she certainly wasn't herself after the baby died, but he still had a hard time imagining his daughter capable of attempting murder.

Carter Mason walked into the jail twisting one end of his mustache so rapidly that it appeared as if the hair was stuck to his fingers and he was trying to get it off them. His face looked drained of color and his shoulders sagged.

"Carter, what is it?" Gideon asked as he shoved the telegram into a drawer.

"I found Lewis dead on the road. Somebody shot him," Carter said.

"Damn it to hell. Shotgun blast or a bullet?"

"A bullet to the chest. I'd say it hit his heart."

"Antonio Cortez promised me that he'd keep his end of the bargain," Gideon said as he rubbed his scar.

Carter sat down in a chair across from the desk. "Gideon, I wouldn't bet the Mexican did it. They wouldn't have known Lewis planned to ride through there unless they just waited him out. Lewis was trying to stir up trouble again. We were all supposed to meet at Andrew Stallings' place. The rest of us were going to try to talk Lewis out of causing any more trouble. We had had our fill."

"Why did he sign the agreement if he wasn't going to stick to it?" Gideon asked more to himself than Carter.

"Because you were going to arrest him if he didn't. You humiliated him when you tipped his chair over in front of everybody. Lewis was a proud man and he didn't forget a slight. You made an enemy, Gideon."

"How did he think he could get by with making trouble now?"

"He had this wild plan of hiring professionals to attack the sheepherders while all of us ranchers sat at the Last Chance. Nobody would go along with it and he threatened to hire them himself. Some of us were going to make one more attempt today to talk him out of it," Carter said.

"So, in other words, you think it's highly likely that another rancher killed Lewis to put a stop to the trouble," Gideon said.

"I don't know that for a fact, but it wouldn't surprise me. A lot of the ranchers wanted no part of it from the beginning. I know I sure regret that I let Lewis talk me into getting involved. We should've waited to see how things worked out with the sheepherders."

Leaning back in his chair, Gideon said, "We better go get the body. If the bullet is still in him, I want Doc to retrieve it with you there. Antonio's men use fifty caliber Sharps. Most everybody around here uses a .44-40."

"Lewis told me that he never meant to kill that sheepherder. The sheepherder ran out in front of

Lewis's horse and got ran down. We had no plan to hurt them," Carter said as he stared down at his boots.

As Gideon situated his hat on his head, he stood. He realized that Carter had more or less admitted to being a part of stampeding the flock and being present when Julen had died. The confession conflicted the sheriff. On one hand, there was the letter of the law, and on the other, doing what would be best for the community to avoid further violence. He decided it best to look the other way this time. "I just hope this is the end of things and not the beginning," he said as he grabbed his coat.

The two men rode to where Carter had found the body. Lewis lay sprawled in the middle of the road with his horse standing near him. A single shot looked to have entered from the side through the heart and into the chest cavity. Gideon rolled the body over and could find no exit wound.

"That proved to be a fatal shot if I ever saw one," Gideon remarked as he covered Lewis's face with the rancher's hat.

"I never heard the shot. I got a late start to the meeting," Carter said.

Gideon stood in the road and tried to judge from where the shot had been fired. A rocky ridge to his left looked the most likely spot. He walked through the brush and then worked his way up the ridge. The location provided a perfect view of the road, but looking around, he couldn't find even a boot print or a spent cartridge. After climbing down, Gideon circled the foot of the ridge looking for tracks and found the ground too rocky for any such luck.

"The killer picked a good spot not to leave any tracks. I didn't find a damn thing up there. Help me get Lewis across his saddle and we'll take him to town," Gideon said as he bent down and grabbed one of Lewis's arms.

"Sheriff, I know you're sworn to uphold the law, but I wouldn't look too hard for the killer if I were you. As long as that bullet isn't a fifty caliber, I think things will get back to normal. I'm sad that Lewis had to die, but if he had gone through with his plan, all hell would have broken loose around here," Carter said as he grabbed the other arm.

After tying Lewis onto the saddle, Gideon and Carter rode back to town with the body. Gideon walked into the doctor's office to find that Sarah had returned and that Abby had gone home. He whispered to Sarah, informing her of the body he was about to bring in. She picked up Sylvia and vanished into the back of the doctor's office.

Doc watched silently as the two men dragged Lewis into the doctor's office and hefted him up onto the table. He leaned over Lewis and said, "You do know he's dead, right?"

"Yes, I know he's dead. I want you to retrieve the bullet. There's a lot riding on the caliber," Gideon said.

"Well, you two go on and get out of here and let me work then," Doc said as he grabbed a pair of scissors to cut away Lewis's clothes.

"I want Carter to witness things. There can be no questions that things weren't on the up and up," Gideon said.

Sitting the scissors down, Doc peered at Gideon. "I think I have a reputation that precludes any questioning of my honesty."

"I know you do, Doc, but I'm not sure that all the ranchers trust me. Just humor me on this, all right?"

"Suit yourself," Doc said as he grabbed a scalpel and made a slice into Lewis's chest.

Carter dropped into a chair. "Damn, Doc, you could have given me a warning," he said.

"You can turn as green as you want, but if you vomit in here, I'll take this scalpel to you," Doc said as he shook the instrument at Carter.

"Just tell me when you find what you're looking for," Carter said.

The doctor worked quickly in opening up the chest cavity and searching for the bullet. "That was one deadly shot. It got the heart and both the lungs. Lewis died a merciful death. There's the bullet," Doc said before grabbing a forceps.

Gideon and Carter walked to the table and looked into the chest cavity as Doc retrieved the bullet. The doctor dropped the misshaped lead into his palm and held it for the two men to see.

"Looks like a forty-four or a forty-five to me. It's not big enough for a fifty. What's everybody else think?" Gideon said.

"No, it certainly isn't a fifty caliber," Doc said. "I pulled them out of people before and they are one heavy bullet."

"I agree," Carter said before turning away from the body.

"Thank you, Doc. I'll go get the undertaker and have him get the body out of here," Gideon said.

"Tell him to make it quick. I'm sure Sarah and Sylvia would like to get out of the back," Doc said.

"Carter, I'm going to have to ride out and tell Mrs. Wise. I don't know her well and I hate this part of the job. Would you ride with me?" Gideon asked.

"Sure, I can do that," Carter said as he made a quick exit for the door.

Gideon dispatched the undertaker to Doc's office before riding out with Carter.

Outside of town, Gideon said, "I need you to get word out to the other ranchers that the Mexican didn't do this. This has to stop."

"I will. I don't think you'll have any more troubles. What are you going to do about Lewis's murderer?"

"I have a hunch that the murderer is the only one that knows what happened and unless he confesses, I don't think I have anything to go on. None of you ranchers will give him up even if you do know. I'm going to get a reputation for not solving murders. At least you can come in and give me a statement on Julen Laxalt's death."

"I think leaving well enough alone is best," Carter said.

"That may be, but it doesn't make it right."

Chapter 27

On Tuesday afternoon, Sarah sat in the doctor's office trying to comfort a weeping Sylvia. After having returned Monday to relieve a weary Abby, Sarah had held the clinging child nearly constantly. Sylvia continued to cry for her family as she coughed up wads of phlegm. After one coughing fit, the child had vomited down the front of Sarah's dress when she gagged on a mouthful of the nasty mucus.

Doc appeared near his wit's end and his hair looked like that of a wild man as he constantly ran his hands through it. Sylvia made it hard for him to concentrate or treat other patients. With Herculean effort, he had managed to keep his patience throughout the trying time.

Pulling off his spectacles, Doc tossed them on his desk and looked at Sarah. "She no longer has a fever and the pneumonia is breaking up. There's really no reason for her to stay here, and this office is ill suited for the task anyhow. The temperature is warm enough that she could travel. We need to figure out what the next step is," he said.

Sarah pulled the child to her bosom and brushed the hair out of Sylvia's eyes. The first time that she laid eyes on the little girl might not have been as monumental as the first time she held her son, but the moment made for a good second. She still wasn't sure that Ethan and Benjamin had come to terms with the idea of adding a new family member, but she certainly had. No one else in the community had stepped forward to take on the responsibility and Abby and Mary already had their hands full with Chance and Sam. To her way of thinking, she was the only logical choice to take in Sylvia.

"Go ask Gideon to fetch Ethan then, but tell him that he darn well better have Ethan on my side by the time they get back here or there will be hell to pay for both of them," Sarah said.

Doc glanced at Sarah. She wasn't smiling and he couldn't decide if she were kidding or not. He let out a chuckle. "God love you, Sarah. You're one of a kind, I'll give you that," he said as he rubbed his hand against his thighs.

Finnie walked in at that moment. He wore a loose-fitting, light cotton shirt that he hadn't bothered to tuck into his pants. His movement looked stiff as he crossed the room. "Is now a good time to check me over?" he asked.

"As good as any," Doc said before glancing over at Sarah to see her reaction. She smiled and gave the doctor a wink.

Removing his shirt, Finnie hopped up onto the table. "I believe I'm going to live.

As Doc peered at the Irishman's back, he touched a couple of burns, causing Finnie to wince.

"Your burns are scabbing over nicely. I don't see anything that gives me concern. How's the pain?" Doc asked.

"Much better. I don't feel like dancing a jig, but I slept through the night finally."

"I'd say you could go back to work as long as you don't overdo things. There's no point in us taxpayers paying for you to loaf."

Finnie sat up straight and sighed. "That sounds like you. More worried about money than your friend. I'm surprised you don't make me pay before you let me in the door."

"I probably would if I didn't know that Mary was good for the money," Doc said, grinning as he tossed Finnie his shirt.

"I'm going to take a trip and find your replacement for you. You're getting meaner by the day," Finnie said as he pulled on his shirt.

Doc patted the Irishman on the leg. "Finnie, I've seen men do some brave things in my day, but climbing into that inferno might be the bravest of them all. All kidding aside, it's an honor to call you my friend."

"I agree," Sarah chimed in.

Finnie's face turned as red as the burns on his back. He started to speak but stopped. Finally, he hopped off the table and said, "I guess I better get to the jail or you'll probably go running to tattletale to Gideon that I'm capable of working."

"I'll go with you. I need to talk to Gideon anyways," Doc said as he joined Finnie in walking across the street to the sheriff's office.

After hearing that Sarah was ready to go home, Gideon rode to the ranch where he tracked down Ethan, Benjamin, and Fuzzy Clark driving some of their herd into the lowlands for protection against the coming winter.

"What are you doing here?" Ethan asked.

"Sarah sent me to tell you to take the wagon into town and get her and Sylvia," Gideon answered.

"She did, did she? We still haven't talked about this," Ethan said.

"Why didn't you discuss it when she was home Monday?"

"Sarah wanted to, but I was busy and had things to do."

"I see," Gideon said, nodding his head with faux sympathy.

"Sarah and you are probably in cahoots on this. You two are as thick as thieves," Ethan said.

"I never even saw Sarah. Doc brought me word. That's a fine thing to say about your best friend and your wife," Gideon said with a condescending expression.

"Don't you look at me that way," Ethan said gruffly.

"You always get indignant when you know you're wrong."

"You don't know everything, you just think you do," Ethan reminded his friend.

"I know you well enough to know that you're not going to disappoint Sarah by refusing to take in this child. The only thing I don't know is whether you're smart enough to be gracious about it from the beginning or if you'll give in begrudgingly and then have to apologize later for making an ass of yourself after you are smitten by a little girl sitting in your lap."

Ethan glared at Gideon and shook his head. "You are a haughty man, Gideon Johann."

"So I've been told on more than one occasion, but since you're a preacher, you have to love me anyway," Gideon said with a smirk.

"I think you are God's test to my faith," Ethan said cracking a smile before turning serious. "Gideon, I truly am concerned about Sylvia having family that will want her after Sarah is hopelessly attached to the child."

"From what I understand, that is not likely."

"But it could happen."

"I'm the law. You let me worry about that. Come on and I'll ride back to the house with you to get the wagon," Gideon said and turned Buck.

Ethan hollered out instructions for Benjamin and Fuzzy to finish moving the herd before informing his son that he would see him back at the cabin later.

Gideon helped Ethan harness the horse and hitch the wagon before tying Buck to the buckboard and climbing up onto the seat.

After riding for better than a mile in silence, Ethan asked, "So how are you doing these days?"

"What do you mean?" Gideon asked.

In a tone that suggested that Gideon knew full well what the question meant, Ethan said, "With all that's happened to your family."

"I don't know. There's not a damn thing I can do about any of it anyway. I guess things are kind of like when I got back to Last Stand and learned to deal with my past. I just accept things for the way they are and try to deal with them. There's one thing I can promise you though – I may come to terms with Tess's death, but I'll never get over it. There's not a day goes by that I don't think about her and my heart aches every time."

Ethan stared straight ahead and didn't speak for a moment. "Sometimes even for a preacher it's hard to find the grace of God in our lives. I guess that's where the faith comes in."

"I suppose, but sometimes I still wonder if I haven't brought all this upon my family for my past deeds," Gideon replied quietly.

"Gideon, everything is not about you."

Pulling his chin back and raising his eyebrows, Gideon said, "What's that supposed to mean?"

"You tend to think everything is about you. I don't think God is so petty that he punishes your family for things for which you've already been forgiven."

"I don't think everything is about me," Gideon said defensively.

"Believe me, you do," Ethan said emphatically.

Gideon grinned and pulled his hat down low. "All right, maybe I do a little."

By the time the two men reached town, they had switched the conversation to swapping tales on each other in order to avoid any more serious talk. Gideon took one look at the doctor's office door and decided that he didn't want to accompany Ethan in so he walked to the jail.

Ethan entered Doc's office and forced a smile on his face when he made eye contact with his wife. He still had misgivings about the whole thing, but he wasn't about to air them at this moment. "Are we ready to go?" he asked.

"I think so," Sarah said as she attempted to stand while holding the child. She lost her balance and plopped back down on the bench. "Let's try that again."

"Let me have her," Ethan said as he walked over and scooped up Sylvia.

Sylvia's eyes grew large as she was whisked up into the arms of the towering man. Ethan looked down at the child and her appearance gave away how sick she felt. Her eyes appeared dull and her skin color looked pasty, but Sylvia smiled at him and he smiled back. He took in her features for the first time – her blue eyes, blond hair, and pretty face. At that moment, it dawned on him that except for the child's diminutive size, she could probably pass for his and Sarah's daughter.

"Let's get you home. I'm sure you've had enough of that old doctor," Ethan said.

Doc Abram perked up at being mentioned. "I have Finnie and Gideon to deal with every day. Don't you start in on me too or I just might retire and let you all fend for yourselves," he said as he tried to pat his hair back in place.

"Maybe you should take a nap after we get out of here," Ethan said with a grin.

Doc tried not to smile as he closed one eye and rubbed the stubble on his chin. "Just go."

On the ride home, Sylvia sat in Sarah's lap, coughing occasionally and spitting onto the ground. She seemed unconcerned with where she was going until they pulled into the yard of the Oakes cabin. Looking around at the unfamiliar place, she said, "Where's my house?"

Ethan climbed down from the wagon and lifted Sylvia from Sarah's lap. He carried her into the cabin as Sarah followed closely. Benjamin sat at the table reading a book and looked up in surprise at seeing the child in his pa's arms. As Sarah sat down in a chair close to her son, she took Sylvia into her lap.

"This isn't my house. Where's Momma and Daddy?" Sylvia asked.

"Honey, your momma and daddy and brother went to Heaven. They are with God now and you will have to wait to see them again. You are going to live here with us. Benjamin will play with you when you get well and we will take care of you just like your momma and daddy did," Sarah said.

Sylvia did not speak, but her expression gave away her confusion and she hooked an index finger into her mouth. The ride had tired her out and she laid her head against Sarah. She fell asleep in a matter of minutes.

Looking up at Ethan, Sarah said, "I don't think there could be a worse age for this to happen. She understands the loss, but not much else."

Closing his book, Benjamin asked, "Is she going to be my sister?"

"We haven't figured everything out yet, but you should do your best to make her feel at home. Think how you would feel if you lost us and were scared and confused. Kind of like the time you were kidnapped. We all have a duty to welcome Sylvia into our home. Can you do that for us?" Sarah asked.

Benjamin nodded his head as solemnly as a preacher giving a sermon.

Chapter 28

As Gideon made an afternoon walk of the town, he watched as a stranger left his horse in the care of the blacksmith. Something about the man's posture and stance seemed familiar, but the sheriff couldn't put his finger on exactly who he might be. His first inclination was to go introduce himself, but as he stepped towards the livery stable, the man turned his head enough that Gideon could see his profile. Stopping in his tracks, Gideon then eased out of sight. He still didn't recognize the stranger, but felt sure that he had crossed paths with the man before and the encounter had not been friendly. All he had to go on really was intuition, but he had learned years ago never to ignore it. His instincts had kept him alive on more than one occasion.

After the stranger walked across the street and into the hotel, Gideon walked to the stable and found Blackie pulling off the saddle of the man's horse.

"Hey, Blackie, who brought you this horse?" Gideon asked.

"He introduced himself as Joe West. He just asked me to feed and brush him down and to check his shoes," Blackie answered.

Gideon didn't recognize the name, but figured it might be an alias anyway if the man was up to mischief. "Did he say when he planned to pick up his horse?"

"He said he'd probably get him tomorrow. Is there something that I need to know about?"

"Nah, I'm just being a nosy sheriff. I guess I'm thinking this is my town and I should know everybody in it," Gideon said. "I'll see you around."

Gideon strolled to the Last Chance. He looked around for Mary as he entered, but didn't see her. Delta stood behind the bar and he walked over to her.

"Is Mary here?" he asked.

"She's at the house with Sam," Delta answered.

"That's all right. I probably should ask you instead of her anyway. I need to watch the street from your room upstairs. Would you let me?"

"Sure. It ain't like a man's never been up there before, but don't you get no ideas. I'm retired," Delta said with a giggle and a wink. She reached under her blouse and produced a key.

As he took the key, he said, "My, it still burns hot. Thank you."

Delta continued giggling as he walked up the stairs. Gideon entered Delta's bedroom, pulled a chair up to the window, and sat down. The street below bustled with people, and he had to force himself to concentrate on the coming and goings at the hotel so as not to get distracted in a flight of daydreams.

He had sat in the chair for well over an hour, shifting his weight from one ass cheek to the other, when he saw the big bartender from the Pearl West walking down the street. Gideon had pegged him from the start as Cyrus's enforcer. Every corrupt saloonkeeper that he had ever dealt with always had a man to do the dirty work. The bartender made a quick entrance into the hotel. Ten minutes passed before he exited the building and headed back towards the saloon.

A few minutes later, Joe West walked out of the hotel and down the street in the opposite direction as the bartender had gone. Gideon locked the room and scurried down the stairs, tossing Delta her key before walking out the door. He made it outside just in time to see Joe walk down a side street in the direction of the general store.

Gideon headed back to the livery and took a position in a horse stall where he could see the street and the hotel.

"What in darnation are you doing?" Blackie asked.

"Blackie, just humor me. I'm trying to keep an eye on things," Gideon said.

Looking a bit miffed, Blackie resumed pounding a horseshoe on his anvil.

A short time later, Gideon saw Joe returning to the hotel from the opposite direction he had left the place. He found it odd that the man didn't appear to have purchased anything and that he had gone out of his way on returning to the hotel.

After slipping out of the stall, Gideon walked down the side street and into the general store. Mayor Hiram Howard greeted the sheriff from behind the counter.

"What can I do for you today?' Hiram asked.

"Did a man in a derby hat, striped pants, and an overcoat come in here a few minutes ago?" Gideon asked.

"Sure did. I'd never seen him before. He bought a can of kerosene," Hiram answered.

As soon as Gideon heard the word kerosene, he realized Joe West's real identity. Nearly fifteen years ago when Gideon had been a deputy in Pueblo, a petty criminal by the name of Larry Reitz had been rumored to also be an arsonist. They never could pin a fire on him, but the sheriff eventually sent him to prison for stealing. Larry Reitz had come to Last Stand.

"All right, thanks, Hiram," Gideon said and walked out of the store.

Gideon headed straight to the alley behind the Last Chance. Behind a couple of empty whiskey barrels, he found the can of kerosene. He grabbed the container and walked back to the jail.

"Where have you been? I thought maybe wolves got you," Finnie said. "Oh good, we needed some kerosene."

"Do me a favor and finish off the old can filling the lamps. I need the can," Gideon said as he walked over to where Finnie kept the wanted posters pinned to the wall.

"Sure," Finnie said as he watched Gideon and tried to figure out what was happening.

No poster existed for Larry Reitz. Gideon walked to his desk and sat down. He had already decided not to tell Finnie about the arsonist. The Irishman would only get himself worked up into a fever waiting for something to happen.

"Thank you," Gideon said when Finnie had finished filling the lamps.

"Do you want to tell me what's going on?" Finnie asked.

"What do you mean?"

"Gideon, do not insult my intelligence. If you don't want to tell me, just say so. I can look at you and tell when you have to fart, so don't think you can fool me."

Gideon chuckled. "Oh, all right, I don't need your help right now, but I promise you that in the morning that I'll have a job for you and you're going to like it. Go on home. I'll see you sometime."

After Finnie left, Gideon filled the empty can with water and returned to the alley, placing it behind the empty barrels. Returning to the jail, he waited until five o'clock before grabbing a shotgun and mounting Buck to ride through town. He doubted he was being watched, but he wasn't about to take any chances. At the end of town, he cut over a street and came back behind the livery stable. He entered the stable through the rear and told Blackie to put Buck up for the night and to keep the horse out of sight. The blacksmith looked at him as if he had lost his mind, but Gideon wasn't in the mood to explain so he took his shotgun and walked away. He walked down the alley and into the back entrance of the Last Chance. Mary sat at the table working on her ledger.

As Mary looked up in surprise, she said, "I wasn't expecting you. Delta told me that you used her room today for spying."

"I'm going to spend the evening back here. Is Finnie coming over?" he asked.

"No, Mrs. Penny has the night off. He's watching Sam."

"Good. He'd just be in the way."

"Gideon, what's going on?" Mary asked with trepidation.

"Cyrus has hired an arsonist to burn you out. I figure he'll wait until after closing and I don't want him to know I'm still in town. If I told Finnie, he'd just get all worked up and be liable to do something foolish," Gideon said as he watched the color drain from Mary's face.

Closing her ledger, Mary asked, "How do you know that?"

"Luck mainly, but I'm right. I found a can of kerosene out back that I replaced with water. You'll be safe."

Mary placed her elbows on the table and leaned forward to rub her forehead. "No matter how hard we all try to make a good life, there's always evil lurking out there to destroy everything. Maybe I should just sell. This is twice that bad has happened from me holding on to this place."

"If you give in on this, somebody will next go after the restaurant. You're doing the right thing by holding firm. And you have Finnie and me to protect you. Men don't like seeing a woman kick their butt in business. Just think of yourself as a role model for Winnie and all the young girls," Gideon said.

Mary made a snorting sound. "I don't know about that. Will you be able to arrest Cyrus for this?"

Gideon shook his head. "Men like Cyrus Capello don't make tracks. They let their minions do that and they will never sell him out. But after tomorrow, Cyrus will have too much fear of the consequences to ever mess with you again."

"I hope you are right. It's certainly been a tough year around here."

"They all are, Mary. There has been a lot of good, too. Sam makes up for a whole lot of the bad," Gideon said as he sat down.

"You're right. I wish we could have said the same for Tess. Have you heard anything on Zack and Joann?"

Gideon told Mary what little he knew before adding, "Joann is probably in jail for trying to murder him."

Mary laughed. "I seriously doubt that. Nursing Zack back to health may be just what the doctor ordered for them. I need to go up front and help Delta."

An hour before closing time, Gideon walked out into the black alley. Taking a position about twenty-five feet from the barrels, Gideon waited. The cold night air made standing still miserable and he clenched his jaw tight to keep his teeth from chattering. His feet went numb and he couldn't feel his toes. Standing there reminded him of the war when so much time was spent waiting for something to happen and freezing your ass off in the meantime.

Two hours passed before Gideon heard someone coming down the alley. After Gideon pulled his stiff hands out of his coat pockets, he brought the shotgun up to his shoulder and waited. Reitz struck a match as he neared the barrels and retrieved the can.

"That's got water in it now or more accurately probably ice," Gideon called out before moving to his right and squatting.

Reitz dropped the can and match. He drew his pistol and started firing rapidly into the dark. Gideon calmly cocked a barrel and fired. As the roar of the shotgun blast faded, the gurgling sound of Reitz's strained breathing took its place. Gideon struck a match and walked over to the arsonist. Reitz's eyes slowly drooped shut and he took a couple more strained breaths before dying.

Chapter 29

The morning after Gideon killed the arsonist, Finnie arrived early at the jail to learn what the sheriff had been plotting the previous night. Finnie was too wound up to notice how tired he felt from barely sleeping for wondering what might be happening. Upon hearing what had happened, the deputy became so agitated that he started pacing and hopping around the room as if doing an Irish jig.

"So you didn't think you needed me as backup? What if you'd got shot? You would have died in that alley and he might have gone ahead and burned the place to the ground," Finnie yelled.

"This is exactly why I didn't tell you. I knew you would get too wound up. Everything worked out just fine. I knew what I was doing," Gideon said calmly before taking a sip of coffee.

"Why didn't you wait until he tried to douse the place and then club him? We could have gotten him to sing on Cyrus," Finnie ranted.

"No, Cyrus kept his nose out of the dirty work. You know how this all works. The big bartender made the arrangements. I know he met with Reitz, but there's no way to prove he paid him to burn down the saloon."

"Well, maybe we can bluff the bartender into implicating Cyrus."

"No, we can't. People like Cyrus always have somebody willing to take the fall in exchange for money. And even if the bartender agreed to talk, I doubt we could keep him alive until the trial. We've dealt with this before, Finnie," Gideon said. "Now sit down and calm yourself."

"You think you know everything," Finnie said as he plopped down into a chair.

"Tell me where I'm wrong then."

Finnie rubbed his chin and looked at Gideon. "Oh, shut up. I'm not in the mood for your haughtiness."

Grinning, Gideon took a drink of coffee.

"So what's the job you told me you'd have for me today?" Finnie asked.

"After the Pearl West opens, we are going to pay it a little visit. I'll keep an eye on that big bartender and you can go beat the shit out of Cyrus. We might not be able to convict him, but we'll make damn sure he thinks twice before he messes with us again."

Sitting up in his chair, Finnie smiled. "Do you think we can get by with that?"

"Well, we aren't going to run around and brag about it, but I don't think Cyrus or anybody else in the Pearl West is going to making a fuss afterwards. He's not stupid," Gideon said.

By the time the clock chimed ten o'clock, Finnie had fidgeted and paced around the jail to the point that Gideon had contemplated trying to trick the Irishman into going into a cell and locking the door. Finnie jumped up from his seat and removed his gun belt. He hung it on a peg and turned to wait for Gideon.

"Don't you get whipped," Gideon teased as he opened the door.

"I'll beat that dago like a drum," Finnie said as they walked outside.

The two men walked down the street and across it. As soon as they walked into the saloon, the big bartender started squirming. Gideon pulled out his Colt and cocked it.

"Put your hands on the bar where I can see them or we can bury you beside your arson friend. I guess you were surprised to see the Last Chance still standing this morning," Gideon said.

Finnie walked back to office and kicked the door open, breaking the jamb. Startled, Cyrus jumped up from his chair just as Finnie charged in and delivered a haymaker to the saloonkeeper's mouth. Cyrus collapsed to the floor, but to Finnie's surprise, the Pearl West owner jumped up spitting blood and ran around the desk charging the Irishman. He tackled Finnie, driving him into the wall and shattering plaster. Finnie locked his hands together and began pounding down on Cyrus's neck until the blows drove his nemesis to his knees. With a windmill uppercut, the Irishman caught the saloonkeeper on the chin, lifting him off his knees and onto his back.

"Stay down you damn dago unless you want more of the same," Finnie shouted.

"Go to hell, paddy," Cyrus yelled as he regained his feet and came charging.

A right hook connected to Finnie's cheekbone and nearly buckled him. He bent his knees before launching his whole body into a vicious shot to Cyrus's ribs. Cyrus let out a loud groan just before Finnie punched the saloonkeeper in the stomach, knocking the air out of his lungs and sending him to the floor again.

"If you ever mess with my wife or me again, I'll kill you next time. You've been warned," Finnie yelled.

Cyrus somehow climbed to his feet again and reached under his coat, retrieving a knife.

"Paddy, you're going to die today," Cyrus yelled as he woozily charged Finnie.

Finnie gripped both hands around Cyrus's wrist and twisted his own body around until he locked the saloonkeeper's arm under his right armpit. With his left arm, Finnie savagely threw elbows behind his back into Cyrus's head until the knife dropped to the ground and the Italian collapsed. After Finnie picked up the knife, he leaned over Cyrus and grabbed him by his bushy eyebrow. With a flick of the blade, he sliced a half-inch of skin out of the middle of the eyebrow as Cyrus screamed.

"Every time you look in the mirror, you'll remember for the rest of your life not to mess with Finnegan Ford or his wife," Finnie shouted in Cyrus's face.

Finnie was tired and out of breath. He braced his hands on his knees for support and sucked in air until he got his wind. Walking out into the bar area, he found Gideon still standing with the Colt pointed at the bartender.

"That dago is tougher than he looks," Finnie said and grinned.

"Or you're starting to get old," Gideon quipped.

Gideon walked up to the bartender until the end of his gun barrel was inches from the man's nose. "You best mind your manners from here on out," he said as he uncocked the revolver.

Just as the bartender let out a sigh of relief, the Colt came crashing into his temple. His knees buckled and he dropped to the floor.

"I believe our work is done here," Gideon said as he holstered his gun.

As they walked back to the jail, Finnie asked, "So do you think we've put an end to trouble from Cyrus?"

"I think he will leave you and Mary alone, but people like him will always be up to some no good. They can't help themselves," Gideon answered.

"He pulled an Arkansas toothpick on me. I used it on him to take off a piece of eyebrow."

Gideon turned his head and looked at Finnie in surprise. "Damn, you were feeling mean."

"I didn't appreciate that dago coming at me with a knife. It's kind of like what the whore said to the well-endowed customer – you aren't poking me with that thing."

Laughing so hard that he snorted, Gideon shook his head and kept walking.

Chapter 30

On Doctor Walters' last visit, he brought a cane, and in his superior tone, informed Zack that he needed to start walking if it didn't want to become an invalid. The young man looked at the physician as if he might be crazy, but the doctor either didn't care or refused to notice. After proclaiming that Zack was healing well, the doctor left with instructions to be walking around the house by his next visit.

The first time that Zack attempted to walk, Jake had to help pull his son-in-law to his feet. Zack let out a groan and stood wobbling with the support of the cane. Perspiration popped out on his forehead as he worked up the nerve to attempt a step. Joann and Rita stood nervously by his side as if they were strong enough to catch the strapping young man if he faltered. Beginning with his injured side, Zack swung his right leg forward and with the cane bearing the brunt of his weight, he stepped up with his left leg. He succeeded in taking three steps before becoming dizzy. Waiting until his head cleared, he managed to make it back to the bed and dropped into it with such force that the frame made a popping sound.

After his first attempt at walking, he quickly progressed in his endeavor. By the end of the week, he could slowly maneuver around the house and had begun taking his meals with the family. The dining had been awkward for all of them at first with no one sure as to which topics to discuss, but the discomfort had faded away until the gatherings were a lively affair full of laughter and merriment.

Zack and Joann never discussed their crying in bed together and made a point not to mention Tess or Colorado. Both of them needed a respite from the grief and worries they had been living under. Instead, they settled into their old routines of acting like a married couple even if neither acknowledged the change or even so much as held hands.

Rita and Joann began clearing the table after breakfast Friday morning. Jake walked to the barn to feed the horses and Zack made his first journey out onto the porch to get some fresh air.

As Joann carried the plates to the wash pan, she said, "Momma, you and Poppa need to go to town today."

"Honey, your poppa will be going to town tomorrow and can get you whatever you need," Rita said.

"No, Momma, you both need to go to town today," Joann restated with emphasis.

Rita looked at her daughter and her eyes grew large as she realized what her daughter meant. "Oh, you mean . . ."

"Yes, that's what I mean," Joann said and grinned.

"Joann, you better be sure of what you want before you lead that poor boy down that path. You'll kill him if you have second thoughts."

"I know that Zack and I are sort of pretending that nothing bad has happened right now and there's no way that can last, but I've come to realize that Zack needs me. I guess I was too concerned about myself to ever notice. It's kind of nice knowing that I'm needed. I think I need him, too. I've made this all about me and my suffering, and I don't want to do that anymore. We need to get through this together."

Rita reached up and laid her hand against Joann's cheek. "Good for you. I think you'll be much happier."

"I know. Sometimes I get to thinking that the world revolves around me and I'm old enough to know better."

Leaning forward, Rita whispered, "Zack is going to need a bath. We've avoided that awkward situation about as long as we can."

"Momma, I know how to heat water. We'll be fine."

"But I don't know if he can get out of the tub by himself and you won't be much help."

"Oh, I'll be plenty of help. If what I'm going to show him doesn't get him out of that thing, he can stay there until the water gets so cold that his manhood shrivels away."

Rita burst into laughter and shook her head. "You are embarrassing me. I don't know what that boy ever saw in you. He certainly is a glutton for punishment."

"I make it worth his while. Blame Sarah back in Colorado. She made me this way," Joann said and winked.

Turning red, Rita headed out the door and walked to the barn. "Jake, we have to go to town," she said.

"I don't have time to go to town. I've got things that need done around here," Jake said as he tossed the feeding scoop into the bin.

"Unless you want that daughter of yours living with us forever, you'll go to town with me. Come on in the house and change your clothes."

Jake looked at his wife and nodded his head though he still didn't have a clue to what might be going on. He dutifully followed his wife to the house.

"Momma and Poppa are going to town," Joann announced to Zack as her parents put on their coats.

Joann watched the discomfort spread over Zack's face. He began acting as awkward and shy as when she had first met him. Clearly, he had misgivings or fears about being left alone with her.

"Oh, all right," he said sheepishly.

As her parents departed on the buckboard wagon, Joann began heating the stove and filling a pan with water. "We're going to give you a bath while they're gone," she said.

"Joann, I don't know. That makes me feel a bit uncomfortable," Zack said.

"Good grief, Zack, we are still married, and God knows I've seen you naked enough that I won't be seeing anything new."

'Yeah, but I might, you know . . ."

"The only thing I know is that you are starting to stink. You can't be around Momma and Poppa smelling and you're well enough to bathe. Your other clothes are clean and you'll feel better afterwards. Now shuck those clothes," Joann ordered.

Once the tub was filled with hot water, Joann ordered her husband into the bath. Zack timidly climbed in and lowered himself into the water, grimacing in pain as he did. Joann wasted no time in pouring water on his head and began scrubbing his hair.

"Your hair is beginning to grow back. I thought you might end up with a bald spot. We want to keep you pretty," Joann teased.

"I guess."

"Relax and enjoy yourself. I'm not going to bite and we are two adults here."

With his head washed, Joann said, "You can wash the rest of you and I'll heat some more water to rinse with."

Zack had finished scrubbing by the time the water was hot. After lugging the bucket over to the tub, Joann rinsed him off.

"I do feel much better," Zack proclaimed.

"That's a good thing. I do prefer my husband to feel like a living, breathing man. I'll be right back. I need to get you a towel," Joann said before leaving the room.

Joann walked to her bedroom and shed her clothes. Pausing at the doorway, she thought about what she was about to do and all the consequences that could come from it. She knew that a lot of mourning still lay ahead, but seeing Zack's own grief for the loss of his daughter had changed her. Her momma had been right that you can't outrun your troubles, and she and Zack needed each other to be whole again. She returned to Zack naked with the towel slung over her shoulder. "Dry yourself off. I got something that I need you to do for me," she said and winked.

Chapter 31

With the weather warming up from the recent cold spell, Doc Abram decided to take a Sunday ride to check on Sylvia. He hadn't seen the child since Sarah had taken her home. He figured that she must be doing well, but he wanted out of the office and an examination of the little girl was certainly in order. The road proved soft from the thawing snow and the horse kicked up chunks of mud as he traveled. With the sun warming his face, he inhaled deep breaths of the pine-scented air and relaxed. He remained disappointed that he hadn't found a doctor to bring into his practice, but all in all, he could think of a lot of things worse than living in the mountains of Colorado and still being able to work at his age.

Chase, the dog, announced the doctor's arrival and Ethan greeted Doc at the door with Sylvia in his arms.

"Doc, we weren't expecting a visit from you," Ethan said as he moved out of the way for his guest to enter the home.

"No, I just thought I'd pay my patient a visit and get out of town," Doc said.

Looking over from the stove, Sarah said, "It's funny how you always seem to show up at mealtime. The chicken is just about fried."

Pulling off his hat, Doc said, "I'm old, but I'm not a fool, and I make no bones about trying to wrangle a meal out of you."

"Come over here and talk to me while Ethan and Benjamin finish their game of checkers," Sarah said.

Doc shuffled over to the kitchen. "So how is Sylvia doing?" he asked.

"She's getting better every day. She still has some coughing fits, but nothing like before."

"That's good to hear. Sounds like her lungs are healing. How is the rest of it going?" Doc asked in a confidential tone.

Looking over, Sarah smiled. "Sylvia is a bit clingy right now. When she and I are here alone, I can hardly get things done for her, and once Ethan comes home, she is glued to his lap. We've also gained a bed partner. She's been having nightmares and it's just easier to have her with us."

"That should all get better in time. She's been through a traumatic thing," Doc said before lowering his voice. "Is Ethan smitten?"

Sarah grinned and looked over to where Ethan and Benjamin sat deep in concentration over their game. "I think we all are. Sylvia really is a delight. She can say some of the cutest things. And Benjamin is so much like his father that it hurts. He has this sense of duty to be her big brother. It gets downright comical watching them sometimes. He's also making sure we still know that we have a son. Before Sylvia got here, he was always off reading somewhere or doing something else, but now he has a new found interest in playing checkers with his pa and helping me cook and plan the planting of a garden next spring."

"Glad to hear it," Doc said and chuckled.

"Dinner is just about ready. Benjamin get the table set," Sarah announced.

Benjamin begrudgingly left the game of checkers to begin setting the table while Sarah brought over the food.   After they prepared the table, Ethan said the blessing and they passed the food. The conversation lagged as Doc attacked a chicken leg as if starved.

"Mary's Place is a fine restaurant, but nobody can compare to you, Sarah," Doc finally said.

As he buttered a roll, Ethan asked, "Has Gideon found out anything about what happened to Lewis Wise?"

"Not that I've heard," Doc answered.

"I'm just glad all the ranchers left me out of that mess. I don't know if they didn't think I was big enough to matter or knew that a preacher wouldn't attack a sheepherder," Ethan mused.

"You have a bigger ranch than some of those involved. Everybody knows that you wouldn't take part in anything underhanded. Some of the others should have known right from wrong, too," Doc said.

"Fear and greed can do funny things to men," Sarah chimed in.

Doc told them about the attempt to burn down the Last Chance and the aftermath.

As Sarah passed Doc the platter of chicken, she said, "Poor Mary, somebody seems to always try to ruin her life. That woman has already had a lifetime of tragedy in her short time here on earth. Thank goodness Gideon and Finnie are there to look out for her."

Chuckling, Doc said, "That's true, but Mary has done her fair share of looking out for those two, too. Mary is a good one. I don't know what we'd do without her."

Once the meal was finished, Doc turned his attention to Sylvia. Some of the scabs on her arm had begun to flake off and show pink new skin.

"Does your arm hurt?" Doc asked.

"It itches," Sylvia said.

"Well, don't scratch it or you'll get sick again," Doc said gruffly to make his point to prevent scarring.

After retrieving his stethoscope from his bag, the doctor began listening to the child's lungs as he made her take deep breaths.

Doc pulled the instrument out of his ears and dropped it into his case. "Her lungs are healing. I hear just a little congestion. She'll be good as new in no time," he announced.

Sarah had watched the examination intently. She smiled at the doctor and swiped her eyes. "I'm so happy," she said.

Doc looked up at Ethan towering over him. "So, Ethan, is she a keeper?"

Ethan smiled sagely. "Yeah, she's a keeper, Doc."

Chapter 32

Carter Mason strolled into the jail looking calmer than Gideon had seen him in a long time. The rancher wasn't even bothering to twirl his mustache. With his long strides, he quickly crossed the room and sat down in front of the desk.

"Carter, you're looking well. What brings you to town?" Gideon asked.

Slouching in his chair, Carter stretched out his legs. "I talked to several ranchers this weekend and told them about the caliber of the bullet that killed Lewis. Nobody seemed to suspect the Mexican anyways. I don't expect any more trouble," he said.

"So, did some ranchers get together and decide that Lewis had to go?"

"Sheriff, I don't rightly know. If they did, they left me out of it and are keeping the decision to themselves. Which suits me just fine."

Gideon rubbed his forehead and sighed. "The only way I'm going to solve the murder is if somebody talks because there certainly wasn't any evidence left there. Carter, if you know the killer, you need to tell me."

"I don't have a clue, though I still think a rancher did it, but nobody's going to be talking. You are not going to solve Lewis's murder. Somethings are better left as is," Carter said in a matter-of-fact way.

"Come election time, I'll never hear the end of how I never solved the murder of a prominent citizen of the county," Gideon lamented.

"You kept a war from breaking out. That has to count for something."

"Do you think the peace will hold?"

"I do until more sheepherders start coming. It sounds like they're thicker than lice out in California. More will be coming this way."

Shoving a piece of paper and a pen towards the rancher, Gideon said, "Write down what Lewis told you concerning the death of Julen Laxalt and then sign and date it."

Once Carter finished writing his testimony, he shoved the paper across the desk and placed the pen in the inkwell. He stood and began twirling his mustache. "I need to get back to ranching. I've found I'm not cut out for all this excitement."

After Carter walked out, Gideon began reading the rancher's note. The door opened and the sheriff looked up expecting that Carter had returned. Instead, he saw the postmaster walking towards him carrying a letter.

"Sheriff, I received a letter addressed to Lyman Dozier and I brought it right over as you requested," the postmaster said.

As Gideon grasped the letter, he could feel his whole body go weak. He had hoped with all his being that he would never receive anything from Sylvia's family back east.

"Thank you, Charlie. I'll take care of it," Gideon said and waited for the postmaster to leave.

Staring at the envelope, he didn't want to open it. The postmark was from Pennsylvania and the handwriting looked crude and uneven. Gideon rubbed his scar as he leaned back in his chair and took a deep breath. He blew his cheeks up as he exhaled loudly.

Sometimes he hated his job. Everything lately seemed like a compromise of some sort or the other. Garnering his will, he tore the envelope open and read the letter. The note came from Lyman's brother and the grammar and spelling were atrocious. Gideon read the letter twice before shoving it back into the envelope. The gist of letter was a plea for money.

He arose from his chair and paced the room, debating the quandary he found himself facing. He could follow the law and break the hearts of some of his dearest friends or he could choose to do what in his heart he felt would be best for the child. Since becoming sheriff, he had tried to follow the law to the letter and he believed doing such was necessary for a functioning society. He also knew that if faced with similar circumstances that he would want to know the truth about his family. On the other hand, he couldn't get the image of seeing the devastation on Sarah's face upon learning she would have to give up Sylvia. He paced the room a couple of more times before sitting down and writing a letter to Lyman's brother.

Gideon addressed the envelope as Doc and Finnie walked into the jail to get him to go eat lunch.

"What are you up to?" Finnie asked as he watched Gideon seal the letter.

"A letter came in from Sylvia's uncle in Pennsylvania. I just finished writing him back," Gideon said.

The shoulders of both men sagged and they dropped into chairs facing Gideon.

Doc pulled off his spectacles and rubbed his chin. "What did you tell him?" he asked.

Leaning back in his chair, Gideon said, "All three of us like things to be black or white, right or wrong. And lately it's been getting all mixed together in an ugly gray. The way I see it, there's right by the law and right by common sense, and they are not always the same thing. I wrote him that only Sylvia survived the fire. Our newspaper reported that. His letter was a plea to his brother for money, and he didn't strike me as a suitable guardian for the child. I said that she died a couple of days later. It may be wrong what I did, but I chose a place where I know she'll be loved and cared for over the unknown. As far as I'm concerned, Sylvia has made her last journey home."

Finnie leaned back in his chair and ran his hands through his hair and Doc let out a sigh.

"Gideon, I believe with all my heart that you are doing the right thing," Doc said.

"Me too," Finnie added.

Striking a match, Gideon picked up the letter that the postmaster had brought him and set it ablaze. He tossed it in the wastebasket as the flames consumed the paper. "The three of us will take this to our graves. I'll not have Ethan and Sarah feeling guilty for my actions," he said.

Doc and Finnie both nodded their heads.

"Let's go to lunch. Maybe Mary can sit with us. She's a whole lot prettier than you two," Gideon said as he picked up his hat and situated it on his head.

About the Author

Duane Boehm is a musician, songwriter, and author. He lives on a mini-farm with his wife and an assortment of dogs. Having written short stories throughout his lifetime, he shared them with friends and with their encouragement began his journey as a novelist. Please feel free to email him at boehmduane@gmail.com or like his Facebook Page www.facebook.com/DuaneBoehmAuthor.

Made in the USA
Middletown, DE
05 March 2021